THE CHINA COIN

'Leah shook her head . . . No, she wasn't going home. She was just ducking into a strange and probably hostile country to finish what Dad had started . . .'

As Leah steps into China with her mother Joan, loaded with her father's obsession about the blackened fragment of an ancient coin, Leah finds a vast and bewildering land. Everything is shifting. It's a country of adventure, surprise and change. But it's also 1989 – and while they both journey across China searching for the family they've never known, the students begin to march in their thousands. Something is happening – something that draws Leah and Joan slowly but surely towards the terror of Tiananmen Square . . .

And what about the broken coin now? Will Leah ever find out its secrets?

The China Coin was shortlisted for the 1992 Guardian Children's Fiction Award and the 1992 SA Festival Award for Literature. It has also been named a Children's Book Council of Australia Notable Book 1992 and was winner of the 1992 Multicultural Children's Literature Award.

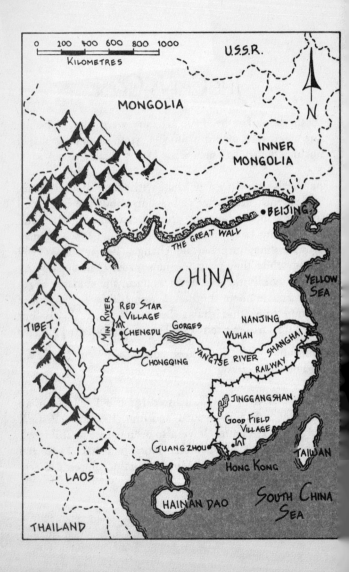

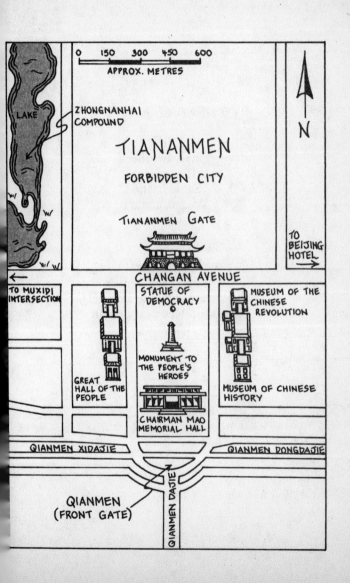

THE CHINA COIN

Allan Baillie

Puffin Books

Puffin Books
Penguin Books Australia Ltd
487 Maroondah Highway, PO Box 257
Ringwood, Victoria 3134, Australia
Penguin Books Ltd
Harmondsworth, Middlesex, England
Viking Penguin, A Division of Penguin Books USA Inc.
375 Hudson Street, New York, New York 10014, USA
Penguin Books Canada Limited
10 Alcorn Avenue, Toronto, Ontario, Canada M4V 1E4
Penguin Books (N.Z.) Ltd
182-190 Wairau Road, Auckland 10, New Zealand

First published by Penguin Books Australia, 1991
Published by arrangement with Blackie and Son Ltd, Great Britain
Published in Great Britain in 1991 by Blackie and Son Ltd
7 Leicester Place, London WC2H 7BP
Published in Puffin, 1992

10 9 8 7 6 5

Typeset in Bembo by CentraCet, Cambridge
Made and printed in Australia by Australian Print Group,
Maryborough, Victoria

National Library of Australia
Cataloguing-in-Publication data:

Baillie, Allan, 1943-
The China coin.

ISBN 0 14 034753 4.

I. Title
A823.3

I wish to thank the many people in China and in Australia who have helped me write and check this book, often at risk to themselves.

This work was assisted by a writer's fellowship from the Australia Council, the Federal Government's arts funding and advisory body.

1 Coin

Leah thought: Here I am, about to be sold into slavery in the lost mountains of China.

The plane dipped a little.

I am being taken to a village so primitive they file their teeth and eat meat raw. I have been kidnapped by an evil aunt, who flies a broom on a full moon . . .

Leah felt a slight tightening in her throat and glanced at the woman sleeping beside her.

Let's stop frightening ourselves, all right? Enough, enough. Sorry, Mum – Joan. Was only kidding.

Leah reached across and dipped into her mother's bag for the ring box, opening it in her lap. She pulled out a piece of dark metal, no bigger than her thumb, and lifted it to the light.

Don't worry about Joan's family hunt, just keep thinking how it was when Dad first laid his hands on this piece of metal. Before the grief and the madness. Before Mum had the letter translated, when they knew nothing about anything.

'I tell you, this is something great, lass. A key, a treasure, a secret – who knows?' And he sat on the couch turning the piece of metal, his eyes gleaming. At that moment Dad stopped being a car sales executive. He was Marco Polo, Indiana Jones, an adventurer with a priceless ruby from a lost city in his hands. You could feel the electricity in the room.

Oh sure, it was not a ruby. It looked like a piece of blackened junk. It was half-round – no not even that, *almost* half-round – and it was sheered across its face, as if it had been chopped in two a long time ago. Indecipherable bumps and pits on one face, and a mystery on the other: a few raised lines, an angle jutting from the cut, a snake – if it was a snake – winding round a rod and three tall crosses.

It was not a ruby, but Dad made them feel it was. That was what counted.

And when Joan had the letter – the last letter from her father – translated, it was almost as good as a ruby. The piece of metal was half an ancient coin with a secret.

The plane lurched, pitching the half-coin from Leah's hand to the Chinese hostess coming down the aisle.

'Rough weather.' The hostess smiled as she passed the coin back to Leah.

'Thank you very much.' Leah gripped it.

'Oh, it's broken.' The hostess looked over Leah's shoulder.

'It's all right. It's always been broken. At least since we've had it.'

'It looks old, very old. Is it from China?'

Leah nodded. 'The other part of the coin is still in China – supposed to be.'

'Ah, you're coming home.'

'I've never been in China before.' Leah let a sliver of coldness slip into her voice. She's looking at my hair, Leah thought. Not the rest of me.

'Doesn't matter, you're coming home. Good luck.' The seat belt lights blinked on and the hostess moved away.

Leah shook her head. Couldn't the woman see? She was not Chinese, not even an ABC – Australian born Chinese. Joan was Chinese, all right,

10

but Dad, David Waters, had been English. Didn't it show?

She touched her cheek, as if to check that her freckles were still there.

No, she wasn't going home. She was just ducking into a strange and probably hostile country to finish what Dad had started. Simple as that. And Joan . . .

The lights of Guangzhou slid out of the black and washed over Joan's face.

Leah was touched by a moment of uncertainty. She studied her sleeping mother, black hair wisped with grey, high cheekbones and the lips pressed lightly together. A Chinese woman, but she was wearing a Swiss watch, a New Zealand blouse, an Australian skirt, English walking shoes, with an American magazine on her lap. And everyone thought she sounded English.

Joan had been trying hard since the coin had arrived, but she just wasn't Chinese. Not a *real* Chinese, not a China Chinese. Born in Penang, given her name after Saint Joan by the nuns in the convent in Singapore where she was educated. Moved to Sydney when she was still a teenager. No, Joan wasn't going home to China. Definitely not.

But that half-coin was pulling them both into China. Separately.

For Joan the coin was the key to a lost family. She had not known these people existed before the coin, but now they had become all the family she had. She *had* to find them and Leah thought she understood that much. If that was all it was . . .

They were all the family Leah had, but she wasn't involved in that. Not really. Let Joan find her family. She was going for Dad.

Long after the letter had been read, he'd been hunching over the coin, holding his glasses like a magnifying glass over it, nodding as if it was speaking to him. 'Were you cut by a sword? Why? When? What do you mean? Do you signify some terrible conflict? What are you?' Then he looked up at her. 'Oh, we are lucky, lass. Most people inherit money. Poor people. When it's gone there's nothing left. But we inherit a mystery, a challenge. We must go. All of us. To find out the secret of the coin.'

Dad was not here. The three were now two, but Dad's last adventure did not have to be over. Not as long as there was someone around to keep it going . . .

Leah turned the coin in her fingers as the plane bounced on the runway.

Joan sighed awake. 'In China, are we? Excited?'

'Tired.' Leah put the coin back in the ring box and was surprised to see a slight tremor in her hand.

Joan caught the hand and squeezed it. 'It won't be so bad. You'll see.' But there was a tremor in her grip.

The plane slowed and turned back to the terminal. The passengers shuffled into the aisles, swinging bags down from the overhead lockers. Leah clicked her seat belt off and stepped into the crush. A small man hit her on the head with a briefcase. A muttering woman lurched into her. Joan threw a bag at her and waved her off.

The hostess smiled at her as she stepped toward the open door, and said: 'Welcome home.'

She hesitated and thought hollowly: They are waiting for you . . .

Joan placed her hand on Leah's shoulder and they stepped together into China.

China was a bowl of warm porridge. Leah gripped the rail to stop herself from wafting away in the night. Nothing was solid. The gleaming steps rippled down to the grey tarmac. The rail dripped from her hand. Shadowy people snaked slowly past dead aircraft toward lights in the mist.

'Our first discomfort.' Joan smiled weakly. 'There'll be many more.'

As she walked Leah stared at the Chinese characters on the walls of the terminal, alien and faintly menacing.

'It's all right,' she said, but she was not sure whether she was talking to Joan or herself.

Yes, you can read some of it. Those terrible eighteen months of Chinese study Joan shoved down your throat did some good. Says 'Guangzhou'. 'Course it says Guangzhou. What else could it say, 'You are going the wrong way'?

The long line of people ballooned outside an open glass door and for a long time Leah shuffled very slowly forward. Joan alternated between sighing and clicking her tongue.

Suddenly the watchful men in crisp army uniforms reached for their passports . . .

Now we get arrested for carrying damaged currency.

. . . the passports were stamped and they picked up their bags and walked into the street.

Would you stop making a big drama out of everything!

Joan ducked into a midnight bank and came out, counting crisp notes, and Leah drooped and dripped in the still air.

A man with a tired face was talking to her in Chinese, something about a taxi. She pointed at Joan and was slightly alarmed when Joan changed gears, switching from the anxious suburban woman who wanted to be called 'Joan' instead of 'Mum' to a hunched shrew, babbling away in Chinese as if she had never known a word of English.

Not Chinese, but Cantonese, and Joan was on

her home ground. Chinese was putonghua, the national language by government decree, but it was apparently not spoken in Guangzhou.

Joan was repeatedly banging her forefingers together to form an X.

The taxi driver finally sighed and took Joan's suitcase. Joan lifted her chin in triumph and followed the driver to his car. Leah flopped, a wet rag, into the back.

Joan beamed at her. 'Wanted me to pay him in American dollars. Then thirty yuan, but he's doing it for ten. Thought I was a tourist.'

They glided along a raised highway, past grimy old buildings with dim lights and windows opening on cramped little rooms, mouseholes to live in. But the taxi reached a silken river and a tall hotel with a cool lobby.

And when they reached their room Leah could almost believe that she was still at home. Normal beds, telephones, TV, showers, toilets – everything was the same, except for the large thermos of hot water and the lidded cups for tea.

Leah turned on the TV and walked to the window to look down on the river. The Pearl. Once upon a time British warships sailed out there and bombarded the city, so they could sell opium. When Guangzhou was Canton.

Some of the edgy weariness washed from Leah's face. History is dull, lifeless, when you read it half a world away, but when you're *here* where the battle happened, it begins to breathe. Maybe it won't be so bad . . .

'That is better.' Joan whirled out of the shower. 'We are going to have a wonderful . . .'

Leah turned into the room. Joan was standing in front of the TV, dripping on the carpet, crushing her hands into fists, staring at a small mob in an open space.

'What's up?'

'Nothing, nothing.' Joan opened her hands and smiled too hard. 'Someone's died in Beijing and students are unhappy. Beijing is a long way away. It can't possibly affect us.' She nodded to herself and turned the TV off quickly.

She rubbed her hands together and forced a smile. 'How do you feel now? We're in China!'

2 China

'Cantonese cuisine is the best in China – in the world! Eat, eat!' Joan had been selling China to Leah from the moment they got up next morning. Now they were having yum-cha – a long procession of tit-bits and cakes – on the revolving restaurant on the top of the hotel.

But Leah was taking her first look at China in daylight and she wasn't sure she liked it.

'Have a dumpling! Tell you what, we won't even start to look for our village today. We'll see what Guangzhou is like . . .'

You can see what Guangzhou is like from here, Leah thought.

Outside there was an endless panorama of muddy buildings: being built, being torn down or just glowering in the heat. The sky was still and grey and maybe it had been that way forever. Pearl River? It was a river of lead.

'My mother talked a lot about the great city of Canton. River jammed with junks, always the smell of fish cooking . . .' Joan was gazing, almost

15

dreamily, over the city. 'You see, Leah? We came from here . . .'

Leah shifted uncomfortably. She had not thought much about Joan having a mother. Joan had been *there*, at the beginning, and that was that.

They finished the yum-cha and walked across the road to stroll by the river, which did not get better.

'Why did they call it the Pearl River, Joan?' Leah said. 'It's dirty mud.'

Joan made a face. 'Maybe it was a pearl river once. A long time ago.'

They watched rusty freighters creep past islands of low barges, ferries working the current, a lone fisherman standing on a small rowboat with a net on a long pole.

Leah noticed a few young women looking curiously at her. Always looking *up* at her. I am a giant, she thought.

Before the coin the Chinese were *them*, the intense students, the restaurant waiters, with their stumbling, flat English. Friends said that she sounded like Crocodile Dundee whenever she talked to them, to make sure they understood she was a local. Now she was in China she wanted to pass as one of them, so they wouldn't stare at her, but they were still *them* and she was a giant.

A man spat at the footpath as he passed. A squatting youth waved a bone and a striped fragment of fur at the man. The man waved the youth back and moved away.

'What – '

'Change money? Change money?' A furtive man in a gleaming blue shirt was talking to Joan out of the side of his mouth while he was staring at the striped foot.

Obviously a spy, Leah thought smugly. Wanting money for his microfilm.

The man in the blue shirt made another offer and Joan looked a little interested, but not enough.

Just a minute, this was for real!

Joan was actually getting involved in some sort of crime. A policeman could step out from behind a tree and haul her away . . .

'Mum . . .'

'Shutup.'

The man in the blue shirt made a final offer and Joan nodded at the fisherman. The man in the blue shirt pulled a lot of notes from his pocket, apparently tens. Joan shook her head and began to walk way. The man called softly at her back and pulled more notes from another pocket, this time fifties. Joan accepted the money and motioned the man away while she counted it. She then motioned Leah close and gave her some of the money she had changed last night. Far less than Joan had received and the notes were different.

'Now you give that to the man. I don't want him anywhere near my bag. Don't wave it around.'

Leah stepped stiffly to the man and pushed the notes forward. 'All right?' She said in Cantonese.

The man looked up in slight surprise, then smiled. He moved away without glancing at the money.

'That was illegal, wasn't it?' Leah hissed as they walked past the youth with the animal bone.

Joan nodded happily. 'We did all right there. He tried to catch us with the old little-note trick. You can't count the little notes and he was going to make sure you couldn't count them right.'

'How did you know that?'

'Ah, I had friends in Singapore. A boy of eleven took me along to see him operate on the tourists.'

'You did *that*?' It was as if a curtain was being slowly lifted on a stranger. Leah felt uneasy.

'Oh no, no. I was only ten. I was in awe of the

17

big Long Noses, but I watched. Weren't we a great team?'

'Could we have been arrested if we were caught?'

'Oh, I suppose so. But I don't think the police would bother.'

'What did we do?'

'Tourists have FEC – Foreign Exchange Certificates – and that's all we are supposed to use. The Chinese have RMB – Renminbi – people's money. Some value in the shops, but FEC are worth almost twice RMB on the black market. So we change our FEC with the man, for as many RMB as we can get away with. We use FEC in the hotels, planes, trains, anything run by the government, but otherwise we use RMB. Simple.'

Oh fine, thought Leah. So now I've got a gangster for a mother.

Another man leered at her from the pavement with three large striped animal feet. She shied away, put Joan between her and the animal feet. 'What *are* they?'

'Oh, them. Tiger claws.'

Leah stopped in horror. She could see at least five ragged men peddling claws on the riverfront.

Joan pulled her along. 'Don't worry. Those types of tigers are caught in the back streets of Singapore too. Supposed to be magic for your health, but they're fakes. Made of cow bones, I think. But that reminds me. I want something for *my* old bones.'

'Where are we going?'

'To market, to market, to buy a – a lot things. Come on, this is going to be an education. My mother talked a lot about Qingping Market.'

Qingping Market was a long walk away. A long walk through hurrying crowds, sticky heat and a clinging stink of petrol fumes, old cooked food, brick dust and a trace of sewage. They skipped through a torrent of bikes on the road and edged past long lanes of bikes parked on the pavement. An old man smiled at Leah as he slowly pedalled by, a mighty tower of boxes wobbling over his head. A little later she was clucked at for getting in the way of a man riding along carrying hens rammed in cages, cages jammed on top of each other, and bound hens dangling outside the cages, beaks almost scraping the road.

'That's cruel.' Leah wanted to push the man off his bike.

'You can't change anything,' Joan said.

Leah found the market a relief. Off the road into a covered lane, a clutter of dried things, stacked, hanging from hooks. The air carried a tantalising tickle of salt, hops, dusty herbs, ginger and a touch of fish. She followed Joan into the narrow passage, dancing around skeletons of starfish, under curtains of musky leaves, over hills of brittle shells. Joan stopped and bought something that looked like a horn made of woven grass, but wasn't. She bought a fragment of a tree root and something that might have come from a vegetable or an animal a long time ago.

'What are those, Joan?'

'Ancient Chinese medicine.'

'Oh. Like the tiger paws.'

'Not like that at all. This works. Has worked for hundreds of years. For my back. Come on.'

The crowded, aromatic lane opened to a broad street, covered in green and white panels. There were many people looking over loaded stalls but the market was not yet crowded. Caged kittens rolled over each other in silent desperation. A white puppy crawled over a carpet of other puppies, pushed its nose through the bars of its cage and looked sadly at Leah. Old-faced monkeys hung on their cages and stared into space.

'Pet shop?'

'No. No pets. We don't want anything here. We leave.'

A large lizard, a salamander, broke from its tub of water and bolted for freedom. Two men shouted and ran after it. The salamander was caught quickly and thrown back into the tub. A wire grid was slammed down over the tub and another cage was shoved on top of the grid. Sluggish fish swam in other tubs. Leah walked past cages containing wild birds and a few racoons. But she was not certain what sort of market this was, until she saw the butcher working with his cleaver.

That night Joan took Leah to a pavement restaurant near the hotel. Leah didn't feel like eating, especially after seeing the restaurant, but Joan insisted. 'It'll educate you,' she said. Everything that was unpleasant, ugly or revolting about Guangzhou was 'educating'.

The restaurant was a hole in the corner of an old grey building. There was a stove with a huge blackened wok facing the street, billowing smoke and fumes out over the pavement and back into the restaurant. A grimy fish tank and a closed basket reduced the entrance to a totter and a hop. There were a few tables in the restaurant and a few more on the pavement outside. Joan picked a table against a lamppost and Leah was faintly relieved. At least on the street you could feel the air moving.

'Well, what would you like?' Joan said as a woman placed greasy chopsticks on the gritty table.

'Just vegetables.'

'That all? You need more than that.'

'Just rice.' Leah looked through the film on her glass.

'Don't worry about that.' Joan wiped the chopsticks, the bowls, the glasses with tissues. 'This is very fresh food. Far fresher than the hotel restaurants. Straight from the market to us. Ready to be cooked for us. What about a fish?'

'Fish?'

'Yes.' Joan talked quickly to the woman and the woman retreated into the restaurant.

Leah watched her approaching the fishtank with a net. There were two fish in the tank. Leah raised her hand and there was one fish in the tank and there was nothing she could say.

A few minutes later she was approached by a grimy little girl with large eyes and her open hand stretched out. There was a grimier man standing in the shadows behind the little girl.

Joan saw the girl and lifted her eyes at the man. 'Go away!' She threw a little money at the man's face.

The little girl picked up the money and walked silently away with the man.

'Thought they had stopped that,' Joan muttered.

The woman in the restaurant reached into the basket and pulled out a small curling snake. Joan nodded.

'You're not . . .?'

'Why not? Good for rheumatism and it tastes like chicken.'

Leah dropped her eyes. Joan was changing with every minute they spent in Guangzhou and it was starting to get frightening.

The fish and the snake were brought to the table. Leah started to take the fish apart with her chopsticks but the other fish was staring at her from its tank. She was not hungry.

'Hey!' Someone had just flicked a splatter of white at her shirt.

A young man with lopsided glasses peered round the lamppost. 'Oh, sorry.'

'What are you doing?' Joan growled.

The youth stepped out from the lamppost. He was carrying a shoulder bag full of rough posters, a pot of paste and a dripping brush. 'Ah . . .' He was fumbling for the words. 'Telling the facts.'

'What facts?'

'Yaobang is dead but democracy lives. Is that good?'

'You are political.'

'Oh yes. Definitely.'

'Are you allowed to do that? Stick up posters everywhere?'

'Oh, no.' He raised his finger to his lips and looked about him. 'We are Enemies of the State. Terrible. Why, if they caught us . . .' He shrugged, but winked at Leah.

'Well go on, be an enemy of the state somewhere else. Go on, away.'

The youth looked hurt but moved away.

'I thought he was nice,' Leah said. 'What's Yowbang?'

'Hu Yaobang was a government leader who wanted reform. Now he is dead.' Joan passed her hand across her forehead. 'That was what last night's TV report was about. It's closer than we thought . . .'

The night exploded. Detonations filled the air around Leah, forcing her head down, skidding her chair back, a glass spinning to the pavement. They were in the middle of an insane gun-battle! Where was that youth?

Across the road, grinning at her. Pointing at the restaurant.

And near the fishtank a chain of large red crackers was writhing, exploding itself to bits.

Joan recovered quickly. 'Celebration. The owner

22

of this restaurant must be getting married. Noisy, aren't they?' She was smiling, but her face was white.

Leah was squeezing her fists into tight white balls. 'I hate it. I hate China.'

3 The Village

Leah stopped combing her hair before the mirror and stared. She frowned at the mirror and the girl with the long black hair, the brown eyes, the sniffy nose and the freckles frowned back at her. Dad's nose, Dad's freckles . . .

'You're not Chinese. You don't even look like them,' she told herself, and looked quickly over her shoulder.

But Joan was out, had been gone for two hours, chasing up her village in government offices.

Dad never said you were English, or Chinese, or Australian. It didn't matter. You were just the kid, *his* kid and you knew just where you were. You lived in an old house in the Sydney suburb of Chatswood, went to high school, played hockey and had a few friends like Rose and Andy – and even a sort of boyfriend, Ben. Dad came from Ipswich; Mum came from Singapore and what more did you need to know than that? It was more important to know how to fix a puncture on your bike, and know that Ben Harrington could and would carry that bike five kilometres on his back if you forgot to carry the puncture repair kit. And that you never, never, called Rose Rosie, and you

23

never went round to Andy's place when her uncle
– Zorba with the hands – was home.

Chatswood was home, where you never made
Andy feel Greek outside of soccer matches and
they never made you feel Chinese, except when
they passed one of those stupid 'Asians Go Home'
wall scrawls, and looked guiltily at you, as if they
were responsible.

Or rather, Chatswood had been home. Oh, that
it could go back to that! Even back to after the
coin, back to Dad trying to speak putonghua and
watching Chinese movies without reading the sub-
titles, back to everything before the Cough . . .

Leah turned away from the mirror.

After that, when it was all over, Mum had
become 'Joan' and the coin was all hers. *Her* lost
Ancestral Village deep in southern China, with her
half-Chinese daughter tacked on.

But this half-English daughter is coming along
to solve her father's mystery. Something she has to
do . . .

A clatter outside and Joan swept into the room,
clapping, her dress swirling. 'We've found the
village!'

Leah looked up from the mirror. Just like that?

'C'mon, we've got to go, go! I've got a taxi
down below.'

Leah rose stiffly.

'Shift! Pack, pack. We're not going next week.
We're going now!'

Leah moved mechanically with Joan swooping
about her.

'Found an office clerk who wasn't asleep all the
time and she found the village, Liang Tian, on a
map, near the town of Xinhua.'

'Great.' Liang Tian, how's your Cantonese?
Good Field. This is too fast.

24

They stumbled out into the corridor and swung the bags into the lift.

'You nervous, or something, Leah?'

'Nervous? No. Not much.'

'I am a little nervous. But we'll battle through, won't we?'

A flash of money – FECs – at the cashier and they were out in the stink and grey heat of Guangzhou again. They slid into a battered black taxi which crawled away. The air was still heavy and clammy, but it was moving.

It will be like Rose's trip 'home' to England. Three weeks in cold rain to meet her uncles, aunts, and grandmother for the first time. Didn't like any of them and they didn't like her.

'You're not excited,' said Joan, disappointed. 'You used to be. What happened?'

Of course, of course. On with the adventure! Village of murderous bandits with filed teeth and a secret. Sorry Dad.

'I'm all right, Joan, just a little tired.'

'We haven't done anything yet.'

The taxi eased from the tall buildings, from the factory chimneys, the dusty shops and the piles of bricks and rubble.

'Did you ever live in a village, Joan?'

Joan shook her head happily. 'Just a city slicker all the way. Born in Penang . . .' The smile faded. 'Then Singapore and Sydney.'

'So you don't know what we will find?'

'Blind as you.' She put her hand over Leah's and smiled, but saw something in her face and took it away again.

The first blur of green in a rice paddy. They were getting into the country now, the grey sky fading to clean blue and a warm sun.

'But that's not too bad, is it?' Joan said.

Flat square paddies, some with a flash of water,

25

glided past. Young trees fencing the road, stands of green vegetables dotting the earth.

'A bit primitive, maybe,' Joan said.

Oh great, where are the bandits?

The taxi rolled into Xinhua, a small town with broad streets, a park, buildings rising in bamboo scaffolds, and a hotel. Built like an imperial palace with lakes, gardens being dug and planted. Joan paid off the driver and booked into the hotel.

'We stay here while we find our family,' Joan said at lunch.

'Good.' That gives us a base to work from, Leah thought with relief. And a place to retreat. Who said adventurers have to live rough?

After lunch they found a man running a three-wheel taxi-truck around town and, yes, he knew well where the Good Field village was. He was surprised when Joan hired him and clambered in the back.

The taxi-truck swept out of the broad roads of Xinhua to lurch along a rough, narrow track, winding across the plain. They passed low, ancient villages, lakes, two-storey concrete houses and paddies. They passed a lone woman on a bicycle with a baby on her back, a horse pulling a cart loaded with hay with a youth sleeping on top, a platoon of geese marching along the track. They were passed slowly by a motor cyclist wearing a florid shirt and dark glasses. Nobody seemed to be in a hurry.

Finally the truck neared a low hill, a break in the monotony of the dead flat plain. Leah saw a village on the other side of a rectangular reservoir, sheltered by a dark green forest of massive bamboo. Some of the houses in the village were being built of brick and concrete and would finish as double storey homes, but others were very old, very flat.

The taxi-truck stopped and the driver beamed back. 'Good Field,' he said.

Joan swayed down from the back of the truck and arranged for the driver to return later. Leah stood in the dust left by the truck and watched some ducks waddle casually toward her. The lead duck looked at her and quacked, once.

'Nice village, isn't it?' Joan waved at the sea of tall green vegetables, rippling in the breeze.

Leah realized she was standing in the ducks' way and started to move. But she stopped. The lead duck eyed her for a moment, then turned its beak away, as if in contempt. The ducks eddied past her and wobbled down the road. Leah was surprised to find herself smiling.

'C'mon.'

They walked toward the village through a shady arch formed by tall green bamboo. Bamboo? More like thin trees. The arm-thick bamboos soared from both sides of the path to meet far above Leah's head with a soft clatter.

A stocky woman with a hoe smiled uncertainly as Joan approached. Joan spoke to her and she laughed and swept her arm over the village.

Joan said to Leah: 'She says there are many Ji families here. Almost half the village.'

Leah had understood most of what the woman had said and nodded bleakly. Mum was no longer Mrs Waters. She was Joan Ji, as if she had never married Dad. Was that what it was about?

Joan asked the woman with the hoe if she knew of any families with relatives in Australia. Leah picked it up by keeping her eyes closed.

'Australia?' the woman said. 'I don't know. You'd better see Ji Yin Yu. She has many relatives in other countries. Is your daughter blind?'

Leah blinked and stared at the woman.

The woman nodded and pointed at a stucco

house at the edge of the village. Joan thanked her and walked across some rubble to the house with Leah trailing behind her.

The door of the house was open, with a painted house demon glaring across the passage. A tough-looking young woman was squatting in the sun half-way down the passage, working in a bucket of water.

'Hello?' Joan called.

The young woman looked up and came to Joan with a friendly smile, but the trace of a frown. She wiped her hands on her dress.

'Hello, I am Ji Feng Hua,' said Joan.

Not even Joan now. This is even before the nuns in Singapore. Feng Hua, Fragrant Flower. And Ji is Pearl. Fragrant Pearl Flower. You forget about that. You'd think she would forget about that.

'And this is my daughter, Leah.'

'Li? Ji Li?' Grabbing Leah by the shoulders and beaming. 'You are family?'

Just like that, Leah thought. You're Chinese, you have been here all your life. Australia, Dad, Rose and all the other kids, they're just a dream.

'Well, we don't really know,' Joan said. 'We want to find out.'

'I am Chou Yin Yu, married into the Ji family.' Shaking Joan's hand, pulling her into the house. 'Please, please. Your daughter, she is very serious.'

'Yes, much too serious.'

Leah was translating the woman's name, Yin Yu, Silver Jade, and she liked it. She smiled at Jade.

'That's better.' Jade winked at Leah.

Past a store room fenced off with chicken wire, a closed door, an open door with a TV set gleaming in the shadows. Out in the sun again. In the centre of the house there was no roof. Just a railing, fencing in the sky. Below, the concrete floor surrounded a sunken square and a covered well.

Then into a shadowy kitchen, and Jade bustled about with low chairs and a table.

'Tea?' Jade threw tealeaves into a white and pink teapot and added hot water from a thermos. 'Where are you from?'

'Australia.'

'I don't know anyone from there. We have family in Vietnam, England and America. You were born here? Not here?'

'I was born in Penang. My father, Ji Lian Fu, left here about 1936 . . .'

'Ah, that was the time of the Japanese. Very many people left here then. Grandfather left for Vietnam, but he came back. But you come from Australia?'

'I was sent to school in Sydney, and stayed.'

'Your husband? Where is he?'

'He died.'

Just shrugging it off. Like always.

'Ah. Very bad.'

'Yes.' Joan pulled the half-coin from her hand-bag. 'My father gave me this a long time ago. Said it was a family treasure and should be returned to its other half. Have you ever seen anything like this?'

Jade looked at the half-coin and shook her head. 'I do not know much about the family history, but Grandfather knows everything. He will return soon.'

After a while Leah became exhausted with the effort of translating the Cantonese in her head and let the conversation flow over her. The two women were babbling on as if they had been neighbours for years. Joan Waters was now Ji Feng Hua, and Leah felt suddenly alone.

A small ginger cat rubbed itself against Leah's leg, enticing her slowly from her chair and toward the sun in the centre of the house. She looked back

29

at Jade in guilt, but Jade smiled at her, and nodded. She joined the cat at the edge of the sunken square, tickled it behind the ear and sat with cat on her lap.

'Hello . . .' The cat stared at her like a little old man then burrowed its head into her hand.

A chicken, a ball of yellow fluff, tumbled past Leah in pursuit of some insect. The cat was not interested but the chicken was pursued by other chickens, leading to a tiny twittering brawl around the well. Two hens strutted majestically through the front door, past Leah and under Joan's chair in the kitchen. Leah remembered the jammed cages of hens on the bicycle, the cages of frightened cats in the market, waiting to become some person's meal.

Nothing like that here. But this was still China, wasn't it?

Suddenly Leah was aware that she was being watched. She turned to see a little girl with a red ribbon squatting half way out of the family room. She smiled and the little girl disappeared. When curiosity drove the little girl to poke her head out again Leah waved at her with her fingers and she stayed.

Leah pointed at herself. 'Leah?'

The little girl frowned. 'Li?' Then she nodded gravely, pointed at herself. 'Fei Yan.'

Leah fumbled. 'How are you, Little Swallow?'

Swallow giggled and beckoned Leah into the family room. The TV, an old couch, a drinks cupboard, a woven grain winnow, an open bedroom door showing a white cascade of mosquito netting. And, almost at Leah's feet, a box of sleeping ginger kittens. Swallow pointed proudly at the cat in Leah's hands. The mother? But the cat was not much bigger than the kittens.

Swallow chattered on as she led Leah past the locked door and out of the house. Something about 'wanting a big sister'. A few ducklings were skittering over the rubble, ignoring them. Swallow dismissed them with a shrug. The ducklings were not hers, but the cat and the kittens and the chickens were. Swallow was showing off the family possessions. The sleepy bullock by the reservoir was not theirs, but the lumbering sow with the eight piglets in the brick sty was. The mandarin orchard near the village was not theirs, but the struggling plum tree by the back door was, and it was so easy for a little girl and her strange big sister to climb.

Some older children ran down a track toward the village, red scarves bouncing about their necks. School was out. Some ran into their houses and almost immediately ran out again without the scarves and with small nets on long poles – something like the line fisherman on the grey Pearl River. The children glanced at Leah and Swallow and forgot about them as they lined up on the concrete edge of the reservoir and started to fish.

Imagine Joan living here . . . Leah smiled and stretched into the slightly swaying fork of the tree. And stopped smiling. This was her family, *all* her family. She might want to stay.

Leah stared at the two women still talking in the shadows of the kitchen, the brown woman in the simple cotton trousers and grey shirt, and the elegant woman in the tinted glasses, the silk scarf and the gold watch.

Don't be silly. She would not be able to live here for longer than a week.

Leah shook her head and Swallow watched her curiously.

And that is a bit of a pity. You can take some of this place without pain.

Leah eventually swung out of the tree and was persuading Swallow to introduce her to the kids by the reservoir when Joan called her. Two men were standing in the sun beside her, one old, nearly bald, with a lightly mottled face, the other young and grinning like a schoolboy. Leah walked over with a touch of reluctance, but Swallow ran up to her and took her hand, claiming Leah for her own.

Jade presented the younger man with a wave. 'My husband, Ji Cheng Long.' Chained Dragon.

Dragon dusted his hands and squeezed Leah's free hand.

'And Grandfather.'

The old man nodded at her, then turned to Joan, and spoke in English, with a faint French accent. 'I am very pleased to meet you. You are thinking you may be of our family.'

'We are Ji.'

Grandfather pursed his lips. 'There are many Ji families in this village.'

Joan fumbled in her bag and pulled out the half-coin. 'Have you seen anything like this?'

Grandfather looked at the half-coin, then flicked his eyes away. 'No. It means something?'

Joan sighed. 'Father said it was a key to a family secret. He gave it to me when I left to go to Australia.'

'And now he is dead.' He nodded slowly. 'And your mother?'

'Yes. A long time ago.'

'Or you would know more about your family than you know now. Your father lived where?'

'Singapore.'

'Only Singapore.'

'We lived in Penang. Before the riots.'

'I received a letter from Penang. Just one. So long ago.' Grandfather looked up slowly. 'What was your father's name?'

'Ji Lian Fu.' Pearl Connected to Wealth.

Grandfather smiled. 'Ji Lian Fu,' he repeated softly.

'Yes.'

'Your mother was Kuang Mei.'

Joan stopped breathing. 'Yes.'

'I am Ji Lian Zhong.' Pearl Connected to Property.

A distant boy shouted and splashed.

'Ji Lian Fu was my brother,' Grandfather said.

Joan's face was changing, a sparkle in the eye, the mouth curving slowly. A little girl before a Christmas tree, not quite believing the gifts before her.

Grandfather took one sweeping step and wrapped his arms about Joan. 'Welcome back, Sister.'

4 Family

Joan produced the letter over cups of tea. Leah wondered why she had not shown it to Grandfather at the beginning.

'Oh, you would like to see my father's last letter. Of course, of course . . .' and she burrowed deep into her bag. She pulled out a tattered airmail letter, the ink fading with age, and passed it to Grandfather.

Grandfather blinked at the letter, holding it at arm's length. 'This is my brother's letter? Lian Fu's last letter?'

'Yes.' Softly.

'You read it.' Grandfather passed it back.

Leah wiped the surprise from her face. He can't read.

Joan took the letter with sudden fright in her eyes.

And neither can she! That was why Joan had delayed showing the letter. Self preservation.

'Well, it – ah – goes like this,' said Joan. 'Dear Fragrant Flower . . . In all his other letters he called me Joan.'

Leah could remember them. Stilted and polite as if he was writing to a customer, sometimes typed, sometimes written in ink but always in English. He had paid to educate his daughter in English and he was making sure she had not forgotten. But she had forgotten what little old Chinese she had brought from Singapore. Joan had had to find a friend to read this letter to her.

And now, after almost two years of study, she *still* could not read her father's last letter. Joan's father had left China with the elaborate, full form characters of his ancestors, but China had since developed simplified modern characters. Joan had learnt these in Sydney University. She and her father had been writing and reading in two different languages.

Leah watched Joan stare at the letter, not really seeing it, trying to remember exactly what it had said. Leah began to smile, then she remembered and looked away.

'Dear Fragrant Flower,
    I am ill. Very ill.'

Joan stopped for a moment and pressed her lips together.

'I do not – do not think I will see you again. I am sending to you my little piece of China.

34

There is nothing else. Your mother and I came from a village two hours north-east from Canton. It is called Good Field and you may find our family there. If you want. It is a long time. This broken coin has been in our part of the family for a long time. The other half of the coin is kept by the family in our ancestral village. Perhaps the parts of the coin should become one again. I do not know anything else. I am sorry . . .'

Joan looked up. 'That is all.'

There's more, Leah thought.

Grandfather grunted. 'He does not mention me. He seemed to be forgetting a lot.'

'I wanted to go home to Singapore, but when I got the letter he had already gone.'

The family was quiet and Leah tried to remember how it had been then.

But Jade broke into the mood. 'Well, we must make a place for you tonight,' she said brightly.

'We're staying at the hotel,' Joan said.

'Oh no, no. You can't go back to the hotel. We have only just found you!'

'But where can we place you?' Chained Dragon said.

Then Swallow ran from the kitchen and banged on the locked door and hugged herself for cleverness.

'Of course,' Grandfather said. 'The rooms of Xiao.' Tiny. 'Tiny will not mind. You will stay in Tiny's half of the house. The daughter of my brother will take the place of the brother of my son. It is quite fitting.'

So the locked door was unlocked and Jade whirled into the rooms while Dragon and Grandfather kept talking to Joan and Leah. Swallow just hung onto Leah's arm and looked up in wonder at

the funny words her 'sister' was trying to say.
When the taxi-truck driver came, Joan arranged for
him to come back tomorrow – after all there were
suitcases to collect and bills to pay . . .

As the sun set the expanded family ate small
paddy fish, salted pork and rice under the plum
tree.

'We are sorry for such a poor meal,' Jade said.

'It is lovely. Great,' said Leah. And she meant it.
Joan seemed surprised.

'You have come at a lazy time,' Grandfather
said. 'The rice is planted and growing, the last
harvest is out and sold – '

'Except for the government levy,' said Dragon
with a shrug.

'Yes. We must pay the government for the use
of its land. It is now too bad.'

Dragon snorted.

'Far, far better than the landlords! But now there
is no work around the village that Silver Jade
cannot do by herself. Chained Dragon and I must
look for work in the town.'

'I am helping build a house,' Dragon said. 'Not
my own.'

'Finding work at this time is hard.'

'But not for brother Tiny!'

Grandfather laughed. 'Tiny is a soldier. He does
not have to worry about finding work or growing
good crops.'

'But he is the poorest of us all,' Jade said.

'They break rocks on his head,' Dragon said
with mischief in his eyes.

Grandfather frowned. 'As part of his training.'

'Bang!' Dragon slapped the top of his head.

'Why doesn't the village do something in the
slack period?' Joan said. 'Make bricks, or weave
rugs, or something.'

Jade snatched at a passing mosquito. 'We have

done that. Chairman Mao said, 'Make iron for China!' So we cut down all the trees on our hill for our backyard furnaces and my mother had to buy new pots to melt down for Mao's iron. And the iron was no good. It was stupid.'

'It was a long time ago,' Grandfather said.

'Not so long ago. I can remember eating leaves from trees boiled with white earth, we were so hungry.'

'That was the communes, the troubled years,' Grandfather said stiffly.

'Oh yes! Communes were when we grew rice on Mao's land for Mao's soldiers. It got better when we were given back our land and left alone. But could they leave it that way? Eh?'

'That is enough, Silver Jade.'

'Oh no! Then the teachers had to leave school and clean toilets and cleaners of toilets came to school to tell us all about Chairman Mao – all the time! School was so dull.'

Jade saw Leah smiling and jabbed a finger at her. 'And Dragon had to march about with a piece of wood and pretend it was a gun and he was defending China from you Western imperialists. He was thirteen.'

Leah's smile faded until she saw it reflected in Jade.

'And Tiny is still marching,' Dragon said. He did not seem to particularly like his brother.

'It is all over now,' said Grandfather. 'The Five Year Leaps, and the hunger. The Cultural Revolution – The Decade of Chaos – and the stupidity.' He looked sideways at Joan. 'It is all over now, but we are poor.'

'Not so poor!' Jade swept her hand round the table. 'This is the best time of all. We have very little money, but we are never hungry now.'

A sudden bright light spilled from the kitchen and a radio blared from the centre of the village.

'And tonight we even have electricity!' Dragon laughed.

The table was cleared and brought inside. The dishes were washed in a basin of hot water in the sunken square and the remains of the food was taken to the cat and the pig. Then the entire family gathered in the lounge, a simple room with off-white stucco walls, tiled floor, sagging vinyl couches, a stained-glass cupboard, a rice winnow and a television set.

'Two signs of success,' Grandfather said. 'A Hong Kong house and a colour TV. If your house has two storeys, it means you have relatives in Hong Kong, with all that Hong Kong money. If you have colour TV it means that you know important people.' Grandfather nodded at the black and white image on the TV and smiled sadly. 'We know nobody.'

Joan lifted her head but said nothing.

They watched a serial about a turbulent romance between an opium-running English captain and a girl from a fishing village on the Pearl River. The head villain was a leader of Chinese soldiers who spent most of his time persecuting the fishing village and almost none in fighting the marauding English.

Then the news. A parade of factories being opened, delegations from other countries being entertained, a cyclist killed by a car, and the students carrying banners in distant Beijing.

Joan was staring, motionless, at the screen.

'What are they protesting about?' said Grandfather, bristling.

'They are protesting about corruption and our leaders,' said Jade.

'Deng? The Boss? They are stupid. Without

38

Deng Xiaoping those students would be starving on a commune, making bricks of bad iron.'

'It is all right,' said Joan faintly, as if to herself. 'They are not angry.'

Five minutes later the electricity failed, but the Ji family expected that. Joan and Leah said goodnight and groped their way to their beds. Just before she dropped the white veil of mosquito netting Leah saw a spotted photo of a pleasant-faced young man wearing a crisp uniform and a cap too big for his head. He did not look as if he broke stones on his head.

'Thanks, Tiny, for having us,' she said, and rolled over.

5 Grandfather

Leah woke to the screaming laughter of Swallow outside her door. There seemed to be a great deal of splashing.

The ducks and the geese are attacking the house in platoons . . . Oh, get up.

She pushed through the mosquito netting, tottered to the door and watched Jade chasing Swallow round the well with a plastic bucket of water and some soap. Swallow slipped near the kitchen but Jade dropped the bucket, scooped her up while she was falling and kissed her on the nose.

Leah stayed in the shadows of Tiny's room and smiled, a little wistfully. Once she and Joan had been like that, playing tag with the waves at Manly beach, and Dad an indestructible old bear. Once.

Joan grunted in the bed and Leah padded back to the sleeping woman. She had forgotten how it was. The time when they were the same size and they could shop like sisters. Both giving so much advice that the shop assistant wanted to give up and go home. Joan caught her once, red-eyed and breaking pencils over a crab-hearted Maths teacher and then she had to stop Joan from storming the school. She was forced to say nice things about the teacher to quieten Joan down! And the times when they cooked together. Dad said it sounded like the Titanic going down, but he never complained about the results.

Leah sat on the bed and reached for her mother's hand, and wondered what had gone wrong.

Joan opened an eye and smiled and said: 'Well, what is our new family doing today?'

And it all trickled away.

After breakfast Dragon rode alone to his building site and Grandfather stayed home to show Joan and Leah about the village. Grandfather said there was nothing he could do in the town. There had been nothing for weeks. Swallow scampered around them as they walked toward the bamboo forest, holding her arms out.

'You're a plane!' Leah called.

'A swallow,' corrected Swallow, banking around them.

'She has not yet seen a swallow,' said Grandfather.

Leah frowned and listened to the quiet rustle of the leaves, the click of the bamboo. There was no other sound. 'Where are they, then? All the birds?'

Grandfather shrugged. 'When the hunger came birds were shot. The eggs were taken. Perhaps they will come back.'

Leah looked at Joan but Joan's face was blank.

They walked up the hill in silence, above the bamboo and the sprawl of the village. The old brown houses shouldered each other between dusty lanes and the new stucco houses were now a wall, a castle, guardians of the winding track south. The pig sties were stone trains running from the houses to the reservoir. Only a few people were moving about the village and they were moving very slowly, like ants in treacle.

'It is not old, this village,' said Grandfather to Joan. 'My father – your grandfather – started this village only eighty years ago. He came from the west and built his house where nothing could obstruct the flow of good fortune to his family. I think he chose wisely. You are here.'

Suddenly Swallow laughed. 'Li, Li!' She ran up to Leah, blew out her cheeks and jumped into a heavy squat, like fruit falling.

'Swallow, that's rude,' said Grandfather. But he was smiling.

'What is?' Leah shuffled toward the little girl.

'Swallow has just worked out what your name means in Chinese.'

'Leah? But Leah is an Australian name.'

Grandfather shrugged. 'In Australia you are Australian, but in China you are Chinese. In Chinese, you are a Pear.'

Joan opened her hands to deny responsibility.

'Oh.' Just so Rose never hears of it. Leah tried to walk like a pear, a bloated overripe pear that had just rolled from the fruit bowl.

Swallow squealed in delight.

Grandfather stopped before several formations of low curved walls of earth and stacked rocks. Giants embracing the wind-blown grass. Swallow ran freely through the formations as if greeting old friends.

'This is the village cemetery,' said Grandfather

to Joan. 'The parents of your father are here, before you.'

Two stacks of rocks and an almost complete circle of earth. No flowers, just dry grass.

Joan squatted between the curved arms and patted the hard earth. 'No writing . . .' she said softly.

'Not needed. We know where the family rests. Your father should be here.'

Joan nodded. 'He wanted to come back.'

'Perhaps it is possible.'

Joan looked at him thoughtfully and stood. They walked slowly toward the crest of the hill, talking as they moved.

Leah trailed before the quiet grave on the hill and remembered the cemetery of two years ago. The formal lawn with the little chapel, waiting for the new arrival. Pain, some crying – she never cried – and it was all over. The cold lawn and the chapel were left waiting for the next arrival, and the next and the next. But this was different. It was as much a part of the Ji family as the kittens in the box. People had died but there was no pain here, not any more, as if those curved earth arms were reaching out to her, welcoming her into the family.

For the first time Leah was thinking of Joan's family as *her* family. Joan's grandfather was her great grandfather, Joan's father was her grandfather and Swallow's Grandfather was her great uncle – if she wanted it that way.

'Something wrong?' Grandfather called back.

'No, it's all right.' Leah followed Grandfather to the shoulder of the hill.

The cemetery gave way to a slope of young trees – eucalypts. Leah sniffed and she could almost see her favourite national park, Ku-ring-gai. Dad had led her through thick bush, alive with bird cries, to a secret cove of dreaming water.

'You like the trees?'

'They are *my* trees. Stringy bark, iron bark! What are they doing here?'

'This is waste land. The government gives land like this to anyone who can grow things on it. A man in the village took some seeds from an official and planted them here. So the hill is his and in a few years a forest will be his. Dragon should have thought of it.'

'All the way from Australia . . .'

Grandfather picked up a stick and bent it in his hands. 'Your father, Joan, he never reached Australia?'

'No. Only got as far as Singapore.'

'Ah, but that is almost as good. He was rich?'

Joan hesitated. 'No, not really. Perhaps he would have been if he had stayed in Penang. He had a good business, repairing and selling machinery. But . . .' her lips tightened. 'There were the anti-Chinese riots, and he took us to Singapore for safety. He had to start again.'

'But he must have done well, to give you a Chinese name and an English one.'

Joan laughed lightly. 'It was not his doing, no, no. He just sent me to a convent school so I could speak English and the nuns couldn't handle Chinese names so they named me Joan after Saint Joan of Arc. I think they were thinking how sweet it would be to barbecue the pesky girl.'

Leah smiled. She was becoming interested in this hidden side to her mother.

But Grandfather went on talking to Joan without a flicker of humour. 'My father, he took your father and me up this hill when we heard of Japanese troops invading China, invading Manchuria. Long, long ago. I think 1931. He told us to go, find a safe place, because there was going to be a war. So

43

Connected to Wealth reached Singapore. I went to Vietnam and we never found each other again . . .'

Leah nodded gravely. It was a good story, good enough for Dad, maybe. 'But no coin,' she said sadly.

Grandfather ignored her. 'But why?' He turned to Joan with sudden anger in his voice.

Joan stepped back, uncertain.

'The Japanese came here, built their fort just over there, some were killed and they killed some, but the village was still here at the end. Father was here, and mother, and I came back from Vietnam to help the village, to help the family. But where was my brother? Through the communes, the famines, through the Decade of Chaos, Connected to Wealth gave nothing!'

Joan's face darkened. 'That is unfair. He wrote – '

'Once. Oh, he may have written many times and the letters never arrived, but he never came back. I tell my father that he is staying away to become rich, that he will come back one day and help us all . . .' Grandfather watched Joan's face.

Joan whirled on the old man. 'He had to make a life for his family out there! You don't know what it was like . . . He watched a mob burn his shop . . . He wanted to come back, but when he was ready it was too late.'

Grandfather put on a smile and patted Joan. 'Sorry, sorry. I did not mean to upset you. I only wish I had seen my brother just once more.'

Joan let herself relax. 'It's past, isn't it? My taxi-truck is coming.'

Grandfather led the way down the hill. On the way to the taxi-truck he showed them a mandarin orchard, greeted the old man who owned the village buffalo, and stepped aside for the woman with the liquid manure from the village toilet. He stopped at the 'corner shop', a small hut at the edge of the paddies, and bought Leah a bottle of warm soft drink. He seemed to be making some sort of point, but Leah could not work out what it was.

Joan left the village on the taxi-truck, leaving Leah with Grandfather, who was immediately more at ease with her than with her mother.

'You like the village?' Grandfather said, pointing a disapproving finger at Swallow, who was peeling a stolen mandarin.

'Oh yes, especially Swallow.'

Swallow gave her a piece of mandarin to spread the guilt.

'It is a good place to live in now. Since the commune is over and we can use our land the way we want. A family buys a neighbour's paddy and turns it into a mandarin orchard. The neighbour uses the money to buy a buffalo which he rents around the village. He does not do much work these days. The buffalo works for him. One family builds our village toilet to collect manure for his fields, or to sell. Families that are smart do well, but families who send sons to other countries do better. Most times . . .'

Leah said nothing.

Grandfather sighed. 'Chained Dragon is not smart. I do my best for him. You understand?'

Leah did not, but she nodded politely.

Grandfather walked through a grove of trees and chuckled by a fragile platform. 'Of course some people are too smart for their own good. One man planted these lychee trees at the edge of his paddy. Good idea? But when the lychees are about to ripen their owner must go to bed with them every night to stop people from eating them.'

Swallow looked remarkably innocent.

They picked their way across canals, trenches, narrow bridges, to reach a lush shoulder-high jungle of vegetables. Jade was shopping with a basket and a sickle. Beans for tonight? A flick and the basket sagged a little. Cabbage? Tomato, pumpkin, sage, peas? Anything you want, and everything as fresh as a new-laid egg.

Jade waved at them and threw an ear of corn to Swallow. 'Tonight will be a *little* banquet.'

Tonight was a big banquet. Joan came from Xinhua loaded with her bags, Leah's bag, a pickled goose, smoked duck, salt pork, two enormous ocean fish, rice wine and a pressure lamp – 'For when the electricity goes.'

Jade seemed quietly embarrassed, but she laughed and joked as the meal was prepared. Swallow taught Leah the *proper* way to use chopsticks as they tackled the banquet.

Dragon said he'd heard that the students in Beijing were holding a class strike. Nobody was going to lectures.

'I think that's a great idea!' Leah said.

'You would,' said Joan. 'Poor Deng.'

'But he's right!' Grandfather laughed, sweeping his chopsticks over the laden table. 'He says it is glorious to be rich!'

6 The Secret

For the next few days Leah and Joan settled into the village and the Ji house. Leah was astonished how well Joan became part of the scene, feeding the stove with straw while Jade cooked, going down to the fields with the sickle for the day's vegetables, scrubbing clothes by the well as if it was fun. Leah actually worried that Joan might like the village so much she would want to stay, but Joan destroyed that shadow on the third day, when she started muttering about long hot showers and something fresh to read. Then Leah relaxed and began to enjoy the village.

She had noticed that there was something going on around the house, some murmuring current, but she did not know what it was and ignored it. Far better to slow down and allow the slow rhythm of the village to ripple over her head. And it was very easy to tolerate the small problem of Little Swallow, who had adopted her for playmate and dumb sister and would never shut up.

'Do you have ducks?' Outside Tiny's room, so early the sky was still purple.

'No.'

'Chickens?'

'No.'

'Buffalo?'

'No.'

'Goose?'

'No.'

'You're very poor, aren't you?'

'I used to have a cat.'

Just before dawn a few schoolchildren and some parents trudged reluctantly to the village toilet. (She went later in the day and tried to hold her breath until she left.) A couple of roosters called to each other as the sky began to lighten and a hen shrieked in outrage as some woman reclaimed her kitchen. The cat kicked herself free of her kittens, stepped daintily out of the box and disappeared. The hens in the empty shed complained drowsily, occasionally flapping a wing, as if to bat the rim of the sun back below the horizon.

Joan was still asleep. She was still a self-confessed 'city slicker' – but she had handled snakes as a girl of seven in the Snake Temple in Penang. That had come out last night.

With the coming of the sun, Dragon charged over to the well, jerked up a bucket of icy water and splashed it over his body, shouting, almost in pain. Jade built a bright fire with straw under the stove and Swallow slowed it down with sawdust at the side. Leah was sent out to the shed to find some eggs to add to the short soup and Joan finally rolled out of bed to wipe and set the table. Grandfather came up from his house to join the family for breakfast, then Dragon wobbled his bicycle toward Xinhua. The tracks from the village filled with hurrying men, then schoolchildren wearing red scarves.

Why didn't Grandfather go to Xinhua with Dragon? Was he staying here because of Joan?

'Do you go to school?' asked Swallow.

'Yes. A big brick building in a place called Chatswood.'

'Why don't you go to school here?'

'I don't think they would let me in.'

'Because you're not clever enough?'

'Well, not really . . .'

'You should go to school. You get the words all wrong.'

The village quietened again. The tracks emptied but they were never quite deserted. A woman walked to the vegetable patch; a man rode into the centre of the village and offered to sell kitchen gadgets; a man with a bell flourished ice-creams on a stick.

'Do you have an ice-cream man?'

'Yes. He comes to the house in a van when it is hot.'

'What's your house like? Is it like mine?'

'A little bit. We have carpets on the floor, and a gas stove, and a washing machine, and a TV . . .'

'A colour TV?'

'Yes.'

'Your mother must know important people.'

'Oh no, no. Almost everybody owns a colour TV.'

'But you don't have a duck.'

Grandfather took Joan up to the roof of the house to show her the view. Something was in the air. Jade joined them, and she did not look happy.

'We are going to have a bigger house,' Swallow said from below.

'Another house?'

'Oh, no. This house will grow. When we can buy bricks.'

The ducks waddled from the village to the bamboo groves as the buffalo shambled to the grass under the lychee trees. The cat rolled in the dust and sprawled on a warm rock near the reservoir as the chickens spilled into Jade's house. Joan and Jade walked away from the house, leaving the doors open, to sickle-shop. The ducks moved from the bamboo groves to the cropped grass the buffalo had left under the lychee trees and looked for tit-bits. The ducklings toppled from the rubble and swarmed into the reservoir.

'Do you have friends, Li?' Swallow was grooming a rag and peg doll.

'Millions of them. All right, a few.' Including Joan, once. Now Street Gangster Joan, Snake Woman Joan and more. Crazy woman. Is the split *your* fault . . .?

'My ma says I am going to have a brother sometime.'

'Great.'

'You don't have a brother?'

'No.'

49

'Not even a father.'

'Look at that buffalo! Laziest animal I ever saw.'

'Fathers are fun. Most of the time.'

'I think it's sleeping on its feet.'

'It's all right. Now you got a sister.'

'You? Yeah, thanks kid.'

The buffalo moved slowly from the lychee trees as a wailing funeral walked past, dropping smouldering joss bundles. The cat came back into the house, swatted idly at a chicken and sprawled near the well. Joan came back to the house, alone, with her arms full. The buffalo sloshed into the reservoir, driving the ducklings back onto the rubble. The ducks, however, marched up the road and into the reservoir, completely ignoring the buffalo.

'Do you fish, Li?'

'Only once, Swallow.' In that secret cove. With Dad. After he got the Cough.

'Come on, I'll show you how.'

Swallow and Leah went into the flooded paddy with the fisherman, a silent man with a battery on his hip and two poles. He sent a minor electric charge into the water channel beside him and Swallow used the fisherman's net to scoop up any small fish or crab stunned by the charge.

Swallow ran far ahead of Leah on the way home, leaving Leah time to think about Dad and Mum and her. She had been angry with Joan ever since Dad's death, and she had thought she was in the right. But from the moment they landed in China, Joan had been shimmering. Now the driving woman she knew, now a glimpse of a street-smart little girl, now a polished, sophisticated woman, now blowing straw in the stove and loving it, now turning her back on Dad's death, now putting her hand on her ancestors' graves. Now gabbling happily away with Jade, but watching those students on TV with something like fear. Before China Leah knew Joan; now Leah knew nothing at all.

She had stopped in the shadows of the bamboo and was no longer thinking about Joan when she heard Jade's voice raised in anger on the other side of a clump. Jade was saying something about a 'coin'.

'Well, I wanted to keep them here,' Grandfather said quietly. 'They're our family, aren't they? You need the money.'

'Not like that, we don't.'

'I don't know where that stupid coin will lead them. Let them stay here a week and she'll want to pay for the second storey.'

'I don't want a Hong Kong house! We want a house that we build with our own hands. We are not beggars. You tell them the truth about the coin . . .'

Jade and Grandfather walked out of the bamboo.

Leah watched them go and wondered if she should tell Joan what she had heard. This was her family, her village and she was happy with what they had found. Was it right to ruin it for her?

She hesitated for five minutes, but the only thing she knew was that she knew nothing and was not capable of making a wise decision on this. So she told Joan.

Joan looked at Leah gravely. 'You sure you heard it right?'

'Yes, something like that. What does it mean?'

'It means that the other half of the coin is somewhere else, and Grandfather was keeping that from us.' She hunched, as if she was carrying a sudden weight. 'So he could persuade his "rich" relative to build the Ji family a mansion.'

'What do we do now?'

'I don't want to move from here. Grandfather is

still our close family. He's my father's brother. I like Jade, and Swallow likes you . . . But I guess we'll have to work it out. Somehow.'

It was quite easy.

Joan sat next to Grandfather near the plum tree and pulled out the coin. She was thinking of some way to approach the old man when he sighed and plucked it from her hand.

'Ah, that coin, yes, yes. Now that I have time to look at it, I do think I have seen it. A coin chopped in two . . .'

Jade and Leah stood outside the kitchen door and watched.

'Have you, really?'

'Not the other half, I am afraid. But father did have something like this. I do not know where it went. I suppose he gave it to my brother – your father – because my brother was the Number One son.'

'Then the coin came from somewhere else?'

'Well your father did say in his letter that the other part of the coin is in the ancestral village. He means *his* ancestral village, his father's. He does not mean yours.' Grandfather was looking at Jade with resignation.

'Then where?'

'Our father started the village when he came here from the valley, but he had not been born in the valley. It is a long time to remember what my father said to me when I was a boy, but I think the village he came from is a place called Gui Tu Cun.'

Turtle Land Village. Putongua, not Cantonese.

'Where is that? Across the valley?'

'Further than that. Much further.'

'How far?'

'Between the city of Chengdu and the mountains of Tibet.'

Joan sighed. 'Oh, that's it. I'm just too tired to chase villages across China.'

Grandfather clapped his hands brightly. 'Yes, it is too far. Why don't we forget about the coin?'

Joan turned to Leah and caught her daughter's eye. They both began to speak.

'But father wanted the coin taken back . . .' said Joan.

'But Dad wanted to see the other half of the coin . . .' said Leah.

And both mother and daughter stopped and grinned at each other, for the first time in months.

7 *The Train*

Leah staggered into the compartment as the train began to move, slid her bag before her and smiled at the woman by the window.

The woman did not smile back.

'Out of the way, wretched girl!' Joan bumped past Leah and collapsed on the seat facing the woman. 'Hello,' she said apologetically.

The woman, dressed in a dull grey suit with a red tie and a red badge, nodded and returned to her ragged grey book.

'Well, we're here,' Joan said with a shrug and started to manhandle the bags into the space over the door.

'Only just,' said Leah and scrambled onto the upper bunk to help with the bags. They had waited two days in Guangzhou for the train tickets and then they had almost missed the train. But they were finally off to Chengdu, Joan's way.

The easiest, fastest way to Chengdu from Guangzhou was by air – an hour or so and you're there. The second fastest way was by train, a couple of days and you're there – tired and dirty, but you're there. But this train went to Shanghai. Joan had kept on raving about going up the artery of China, so they were going to Shanghai to catch a boat up the Yangtze river to some place in the mountains called Chongqing and *then* catching a train to Chengdu. It would take ten days, or more. Tell Joan to go round the world in eighty days and she'd do it in eighty *years*.

But it could be fun.

Leah inspected her bunk as Joan moved to a small table below the window. There was a thermos of hot water in a cage beneath the table so Joan offered the grey woman a cup of tea. The woman glinted behind her glasses and said nothing. Joan gave up and began to read an English-language newspaper from Hong Kong.

Probably a spy, thought Leah. She found a light, a fan and an old wall-mounted radio which crackled at her but couldn't be turned off. That was it. She pulled Swallow's peg doll from her shoulder bag, stroked it and immediately felt sad.

'Will we ever see them again?' she asked.

'Who?' Just like Joan. Never remember yesterday. 'Oh, the Ji family. Probably, sometime. You like them?'

Leah climbed down. 'Except Grandfather.'

'He's all right. You've got to see things through his eyes. He's the family elder, tries to do what he can for his people. Give me a look . . .' She plucked the doll from Leah's hand. 'My mother used to make those for me. Where did you get it?'

'Swallow gave it to me when we were going.'

Leah was looking at Joan and seeing how she might have looked when she was Swallow's age. Bit of a shock.

'Thought you both were tearful that morning.'

'Hah! You almost dragged Jade along the road with the taxi-truck.'

'Well . . .' Joan was silent for a few seconds, looking into Leah's eyes. 'We will keep in touch with them.'

'Yes. We're family.'

'Yes.' Joan said this slowly and canted her head, as if Leah had said something peculiar. She broke the spell by slapping at her paper. 'Grandfather's students are at it again.'

The grey woman lifted her head. The red badge was China's flag in miniature.

'He was steaming, wasn't he, that last night?' Leah relished the memory.

'He was reading the government editorial about them. Now, he must be kicking the kitchen door down!' Joan showed Leah the paper.

'Scum,' said the grey woman abruptly. 'The students are counter-revolutionary thugs.'

'That's what the government said,' Joan said carefully, '*The People's Daily*.'

'The government is right!'

Leah thought, forget about spies. She's a party official. But she couldn't stop: 'Excuse me, but it says here that 50,000 people in Beijing are protesting against the government for saying that.'

'Leah . . .' Joan frowned at Leah and smiled at the woman as she pulled the thermos from under the small table. 'Tea?'

'Students, not people. This is how you educate your daughter?'

The thermos was withdrawn. 'Most times.'

The woman stared through Joan and returned to her book.

'Sorry, Mum,' Leah mumbled.

Joan shook her head. 'You know we're following the route of a great march.' She was speaking to Leah, but watching the grey woman. 'Chiang Kai-shek. Marched to Shanghai in 1926 to trample the communists.'

The woman jerked her head up, eyes blazing behind the glasses, but she said nothing.

Joan looked innocent but her lips were twitching. Leah realized that Joan had defended her by conjuring up the nation's old devil-general and rubbing the grey woman's nose in the memory.

Leah was smiling secretively at Joan when a memory disturbed her. 'Mum, why did the students frighten you? Not now, on TV.'

Joan frowned. 'Did it show?'

'In the hotel, in the Ji house. Just a little bit.'

'Not quite frighten. But I had a bad night in Penang as a little girl and it bothers me sometimes.'

'Riots?'

'You've been listening hard, haven't you? It was the Anti-Chinese riots in Kuala Lumpur and Penang when I was eight. Our shop was burned down and we went to Singapore. I don't like to think about it, but mobs, even mobs of students still worry me.'

'I didn't – '

'It was the anger. They were in the streets with machetes and torches . . . It was the anger.' She bobbed her head. 'Nothing like that in Beijing. Just ignore me.'

'Okay.'

'But I hope the students go away before we finally get to Beijing.'

Several hours later Leah was woken from an uncomfortable doze by a sharp cry of pain.

The sun had set, outside was the gleam of rushing paddies, distant mountains and the wash of a dimming red sky. Inside the compartment shadows slid across moving figures, Joan looking up in fear, the grey woman standing over her, rocking with the hurtling train, stabbing at the window with a knuckle.

'Jinggang!' The grey woman hissed.

'What?' Joan was reaching for her ankle.

'Jinggang Mountains!' The grey woman kicked at Joan's ankle again.

Joan jerked her feet away. 'Stop – '

'Why do you not tell your daughter this, eh? This is where the Long March started. In 1934.'

'I didn't – '

'You Overseas Chinese do not know anything, just how to make money and get fat. In 1934. Red Army marching with Mao Zedong for two years across China. Many, many die, but at the end your running dog, your Chiang is ready to be eaten! This you tell!'

'Yes, yes. All right.'

'All right!' The grey woman tapped the tip of Joan's nose then returned to her seat, her eyes shining.

Joan sat in silence, her face pale.

Leah looked out of the window at the shadow of distant mountains. In China she would have to stop dreaming up savages, gangsters and spies.

In China the danger was real.

8 Shanghai

Joan booked in at a riverside hotel and immediately towed Leah out to explore the city, as if escaping from the image of the grey woman. Leah sympathized, but dreaded the crush of the twelve million people in Shanghai's streets. This was going to be far worse than Guangzhou.

But it wasn't. It was Sunday and crowds stay home on Sundays.

They wandered across a metal bridge over a black waterway clogged with motionless barges, and idled about on the broad Huangpu riverfront. Under the trees children played with new toys, old men played chess and young couples held hands and watched the ships pass. Across the quiet street a long grey cliff of massive buildings hunched over the trees, a few blocks lifted from an old European city.

'Millionaires' row.' Joan smiled. The grey woman was somebody else's troubles.

They walked freely up what was The Bund, a centre for bankers, manufacturers and adventurers from all over the world in the 1930s. Built for the Europeans, not for the Chinese.

'But they're all gone now.'

'Good riddance.' Leah remembered Dad reading angrily to her that Chinese kids had been used as slave labour, prisoners in the factories.

'No argument there. You know that there's a park round here that had signs forbidding entry to Chinese and dogs. What's wrong?'

A sliver of thought. *You* wouldn't get in, but maybe I would . . . That is disgusting, girl. 'Sorry, just dreaming. Where do we go now?'

As they crossed the street Leah took Joan's hand and Joan looked surprised.

You can't keep on being angry with your mother all your life, can you? Not after the train. It's us against the world.

They marched together into the city. Shops selling radios, an ice-cream bar, a man unloading boxed fans from the platform of his cargo cycle, a man wanting to change his money with Joan. Joan not interested. The streets had echoed to troops from France, Italy, Britain, America and Japan but now there were only Chinese on business – even on a Sunday.

The buildings became lower and the streets narrower, often no more than lanes. They had walked from the old European part of Shanghai to the old Chinese sector and now the city was alive. Stalls clinking with souvenirs, barbecued pork in a corner, people flooding down the lanes.

'Tourist traps,' said Joan. 'Grandfathers everywhere.' But she was enjoying herself.

They reached an old tea house in a fish pond and a black-walled garden guarded by roof dragons, the Yu Gardens. Joan bought tickets and they moved slowly along a worn path beside alcoves, galleries, trees and still water. Leah found a small tree, exploding with green foliage on a dead trunk. She could not understand it until she saw a thin ribbon of bark running across the dead trunk from the roots toward the branches.

'You like it?' A small man with tufts of white hair in his ears and a knobbly walking stick. 'It is China. It lives, but it is a miracle.'

Joan returned the man's grin. 'Isn't it, though?'

'See the students? They should come here, and learn. Stop corruption, they say. As if fat officials are something new! This garden, so beautiful, was built for a family of officials four hundred years ago. Nothing changes.'

Leah took a photo of the little man and his tree then Joan towed her out into the crowded lanes.

'He was depressing,' Leah said.

'It's not our problem. We're just tourists. Come on.'

Leah shrugged and smiled as they moved down a lane. Spots of rain were spattering the length of the lane, damping the dust and bringing out the tangy aroma of dried herbs and smoked pork. There was the faint waft of sewage, but after the public toilet of Good Field who worries about *that*? Not depressing at all, Joan was right: they were just tourists, wandering eyes seeing it all.

Leah unslung her camera and stepped into the centre of the lane.

Someone was shouting.

At her? She looked over her shoulder.

The lane was suddenly filled with running, panting men. Sticks in their hands. Running at her.

She shuffled, uncertain and frightened. She turned and saw Joan across the lane, mouth wide, shrieking at her.

She was hit on the shoulder by one of the running men, hurting her, spinning her out of control. She could not see Joan any more, a stumble, and she was running too. This had no reason. It was a nightmare coiling out of the afternoon bustle, and nightmares cannot be handled. Only by running.

The man who had hit her – no more than a youth – was running past her with his eyes wide and staring. His stick was a furled red flag. They ran round a corner and Leah saw the lane clear before them.

Another man ran up beside her but he did not seem to notice her. He pushed his face forward into thick glasses, clutching a pole with a banner ballooning, trailing in the mud behind him. The corner of his mouth was damp with spittle. He looked sideways and blinked in surprise at her. They ran round a corner together, then he pushed her violently aside.

She cannoned into a small store, glimpsed alarm on the face of the woman in the stall, and fell in an avalanche of carved wooden poets and myths.

Four youths stormed past her, shouting angrily and waving short bamboo sticks, making the bamboo sigh with every stroke. But one of the youths glanced at her, and he was grinning. The chase disappeared into a cluttered street, leaving the lane quiet.

The woman bustled out from her stall and clucked quietly over Leah and her fallen carvings. 'Students . . .' she said.

'Sorry, sorry.' Leah began to lever herself clear.

The woman looked again at Leah. 'Ah, you are a visitor. Are you hurt? Let me help you.' She hoisted Leah to her feet and brushed mud from her dress.

Leah stopped her with a smile. 'I'm all right.' They picked up the carvings round their feet. 'What was that about?'

The woman shrugged. 'Students being chased – by soldiers, I think. No uniform, but they have that look, eh?'

'But why?'

'Ah, students want to change China. Some people are afraid they might. It is not your affair and that is why the student pushed you.'

'Oh.' Leah held up a carved lion with a scratch on its side.

'Do you have money to buy?'

Leah looked up in alarm. She had no money. Joan had everything.

'That's all right. Enjoy China.'

Where was Joan?

Leah said goodbye, and hurried back to the lane where she thought she had begun to run. Her throat was tightening.

She could see the slow rain exploding on the canvas awnings of the shops, the clatter of the dangling wooden carvings, the people filling the space left by the sudden chase, the faces of strangers.

But there was no sign of Joan, no flash of her blue scarf.

Leah slid toward panic. 'Mum! Joan!' she shouted.

People turned and looked at her.

She's gone. Gone with the running soldiers.

She began to run again. To the corner, another corner, a street, another lane . . .

Hey, come on. What are you doing? Take it easy. It's only a game.

Leah stopped, panting and hiding a whimper.

Shut up. Joan's looking for you now. Where was she going?

I don't know, you silly little berk!

Then go home. To the hotel.

I haven't got a map!

You can talk, can't you? After all that time in Good Field you should coast it in.

I have no money.

Orphan Annie. Look, you walked here. Walk back.

Okay, okay. Shut up.

Leah walked steadily out of the lanes and across a street she vaguely remembered crossing before. She wanted to ask whether she was going the right way, but did not want to appear helpless. Not yet. And perhaps, just perhaps, she could find her own way home.

Then she caught herself listening for running feet.

She looked around, down a long straight street, a few people idling on the footpath, window-watchers.

Are they still being chased through Shanghai? Come on, you'll never know . . .

But the streets now shimmered with unseen shadows. In this quiet city Joan had disappeared without trace and somewhere out there frightened boys were racing with bamboo sticks sighing at their heels . . .

And it has always been that way. Soldiers from Europe patrolled these streets; when Chiang marched here in 1927 he slaughtered thousands in one day – no wonder the grey woman went mad with Joan! – then the Japanese invaded and the Red Army . . . Shanghai is haunted. It must be.

Leah reached a hub of streets and stopped, suddenly frightened.

A great wall of matting and bamboo reared over her head, twenty storeys high, and curved toward her on both sides. It was the great grandfather's grave in Good Field, a thousand times as big with none of the gentle welcome. A breeze got behind the matting and the twenty-storey wall rippled in anger. Not a wall, not a village grave, a huge malignant god of straw.

Oh, come on. It's a scaffold for a building. Get on with it!

Leah walked across the intersection with her eyes locked ahead.

But you didn't see that on your way out, did you? You're lost in Shanghai.

She forced herself to slow down and paced the next block with her hands damp, looking for anything she might have seen before. She was about to ask the way from a man in dark glasses when she realized she could not remember the hotel's name.

But the next corner showed a street running toward the river.

She stopped, shook her wet hands in the breeze, grinned and wandered casually down the street. Now she knew exactly – well, almost exactly – where she was. She reached the corner, crossed the road to the riverside and looked left at the grey cliff of the Bund. Now Shanghai was as familiar as Chatswood.

In half an hour everything would be okay.

If Joan was in the hotel, waiting for her.

She breezed up the broad promenade, past the ice-cream and toy sellers, past the shouting children and the old men playing chess, over the metal bridge, a world away from old street slaughter and running students.

She strutted into the lobby of the hotel, saw Joan on a couch and waved at her. The fright was over.

Joan touched her temple, jerked herself to her feet and walked stiffly toward Leah.

Something was wrong. 'Hi, Mum.'

Joan seized her above the elbow and pushed her into a lift. Her face was dark and she would not speak. Two floors up, the room door was hurled open, Leah hurled into the room, the door slammed shut.

'What's wrong?'

'You wretched little girl! Where've you been, where've you been?' Joan was hissing the words, shaking Leah like a bean-bag.

'I got confused – '

'Confused? Confused! Do I have to put you in a baby's harness to keep you under control?'

'Let go!' Leah twisted away, panting.

'Don't you shout at me!' Joan chased her, grabbed her, pushing a wild face at her. 'Running with thugs, vanished, couldn't find you anywhere – I thought – You think everything is a game, don't you?'

'No. I was frightened –'

'Should have left you in Chatswood!'

'Why didn't you? I didn't ask to come! It's *your* rotten China!' Leah struck Joan's arms away.

'My –' Joan's hand was recoiling, curling in the air.

Leah felt the hot fingers scoring her face as she toppled over the bed.

For a while Joan panted in the middle of the room, the anger slowly being replaced by a haunted shadow, then she turned to the window and shivered. Leah slowly touched her cheek. It felt scorched; it felt wet with blood, but when she took her fingers away there was nothing there.

'Oh God,' Joan whispered. 'I thought the mob had got you.'

For a few days Joan and Leah crept around each other, wandering among the crowds of Shanghai, pretending Sunday afternoon had never happened but staying very close to each other. Joan muttered something about 'sorting things out on the cruise' as she bought the tickets, and they prepared to leave the city.

In the morning Joan stormed out of the hotel in search of a taxi to take her and Leah to the riverboats, after her shower had run cold, the toilet had clogged, and the hotel had run out of change. And there were no taxis outside. She marched up and down the street and back into the hotel.

'They have all gone. Gone for a siesta. Typical!'

'Perhaps we could phone –' Leah tried.

'The phones won't work. No, we'll damn well walk!' Joan hoisted her suitcase and marched out onto the street. Leah followed meekly.

The crowd on the bridge was dense. People pushing, hurrying, looking slightly worried, a single policeman blowing a whistle at a truck and a swarm of cyclists. But on the other side things were changing. The crowd was spreading out, the traffic turning away from The Bund. For a short time Joan and Leah were panting along the riverfront in almost clear space, then the crowd began to thicken and there was a rumble in the air.

'The road is blocked,' Leah said. Perhaps Joan would stop.

The crowd swelled from both sides of the road and crushed gently in the middle. Everyone was looking at a vacant intersection down the road. A few police idled under trees, gossiping over their walkie-talkies.

'Why don't they unblock it, then?'

A deep cheer surged along the crowd as a flash of bright red appeared at the edge of the intersection. The flash became a banner, many banners in red, white, yellow, in a torrent of young men and girls. The crowd clapped as the banners came on, as the protesters grinned at them, held up two widespread fingers in a 'victory' sign.

Joan stared at the students in haunted fear for half a minute, then she pressed her lips together and replaced the fear with anger. 'Damn students,' she snarled.

But Leah felt she was marching up The Bund with the students, separated only by the crowd between them. The students were laughing, friends with all the world – including the quiet police – and Joan was carrying her suitcase as if she was looking for someone to swing it at. Joan had become an enemy. Again.

A student with a band of white knotted around his forehead was smiling at Leah. She smiled back.

He couldn't be the running boy that pushed her out of the chase? Oh come on!

'What's up now?' Joan glared back at her.

'Nothing, nothing. What do the banners say?'

'Something illiterate, I'm sure. There's "Freedom". "We" – ah – "wish" . . . "We want democracy and freedom." And "Long live the people". The big one, turning into The Bund, is – ah – "Da Dao Guanxi", Down with – it's a hard one that, there's no real English word for guanxi. Maybe "Down with favouritism". Young ratbags, shall we go?'

The main march was joined by another flood of students at a second intersection, swirling banners and flags around a deserted traffic policeman's tower. The noise was intense but it was cheerful.

Joan elbowed through a knot of spectators. 'Where are the police?'

A leader was heaved onto the traffic tower by several of his friends as another climbed onto someone's shoulder and onto the tower. In a few moments ten students were on the tower, keeping their position by hanging onto each other. The leader suddenly pointed at Leah's student and beckoned him to the tower. He motioned another student to jump off, leaving room. Red flags were passed up and waved about as the leader started shouting into a megaphone.

Something about a huge gathering in Beijing to mark a protest in Tiananmen Square for modern China and democracy – 70 years ago . . .

Leah's student waved the flag and saw Leah watching him. He grinned and saluted her with a victory sign. If it was the same boy, he was sharing a small triumph with her.

Leah returned the sign.

Joan dropped her suitcase and slapped Leah's

hand down. 'What do you think you're doing?' she hissed. 'People will think you're one of them.'

9 *The River*

The riverboat was a squat ferry with one broad funnel, too much superstructure and not enough paint. But Joan brightened when she learnt that she and Leah were to be given an outside cabin, with only the bridge above them.

'This is the way to see China. In style,' she said. 'Am I not the smartest mother a girl could have?' She was watching Leah's face closely.

'Oh, yes.' But Leah looked away. There was to be no forgiving, not this time.

But they *did* seem to have done well. They were second class passengers, but since there were no first class cabins they had one of the best cabins on the ship. A small room, cool, with two bunks, a chipped sink, a cupboard, a seat, and a moving view – provided they kept their door open. Below and behind them were several hundred Chinese and a few tough young backpackers jammed in long cabins and along the passageways.

Leah was leaning on a rail, watching the students, as the boat pulled away from The Bund.

Joan settled beside her and tried on a cheerful face. 'This cruise should be very good, don't you think?'

'They don't look like a mob.' She could still feel the blow on her cheek.

Joan sagged a little. 'No, they're not. They weren't. I was remembering other times.'

'Penang?'

'Penang.' Joan let it die.

Leah shrugged and fiddled with her camera. Why should she get caught up in her mother's childhood troubles? She didn't want to know.

She pretended Joan wasn't there and stared at the changing life of the Huangpu River. A long river train – a barge towing a chain of other barges – crossed the riverboat's bow and was hooted angrily. A junk, lopped of sails and masts, putted upriver with a cargo of black coal, and a lone sailing junk ghosted past the anchored freighters and disappeared. A clutter of worn submarines and transports marked old wars.

Leah smiled and clicked away.

Then she stopped. The grey woman kicking at Joan, the running, shouting soldiers and both times Joan was white with terror. Not just frightened, but frozen, staring, bloodless. Why?

A man with grey-streaked hair came on deck and coughed, a shuddering fit of coughs that left him weak and clutching the rail.

Joan and Leah looked at each other in startled recognition. Joan tried a feeble twitch of her mouth, then looked away.

The man coughed through bend after bend of freighters, tankers, barges, riverboats anchored mid-river or snug against the wharves, cranes working over dim holds like pickpockets and behind them tall chimneys flickering a high flame, bleeding smoke into the sky.

That was the start, Leah thought. The Cough. Just like that. Do you go up to the coughing man, tell him he's got to see a doctor, right now? Joan did, to Dad, many times, and he finally went.

There was wide brown water ahead.

The coughing man moved away.

No point in speaking to him. He probably knows anyway, and it is probably too late now. Like it was for Dad.

The riverboat throbbed steadily from the narrow thread of the Huangpu out onto a brown plain of moving water. There was no sign of land ahead, only a hazy sun and the dark silhouettes of occasional freighters.

Sitting on the couch, looking at his feet as if he was terribly ashamed of something. Joan holding her hand but looking at the kitchen as if she was worried about the rice boiling over. He'd got something important to tell you, he had already told Joan. He had gone to the doctors, the experts, and would go to the hospital often from now on. Funny words like remission, drug therapy, but: 'Leah, I'm afraid I've got a touch of cancer.' And then the silence, until: 'Oh, but they can fix it, can't they? Cut it out.' Little girls still believed in Santa. But he just looked at you with sad sympathy in his eyes and shrugged a little. *He* felt sorry for *you* . . .

'Are we in the Yangtze now?' Joan asked Leah with a fading smile. 'Or are we at sea?'

Leah stared at the water and Joan sighed and went off to make herself a cup of tea.

And when it was all over, she turned around and clapped her hands and said, 'Now for China.' Like Dad was a TV show: it's over, forget about him. Let's see the movie.

Leah watched bleakly as both banks of the river slid below the horizon and a breeze whipped the water. The riverboat slowly passed an iron island, motorless metal barges loaded with coal clustered round a heaving tug. The riverboat and the tug hooted bleakly at each other as they drew apart.

There was nothing to see now. There was no

China, no David Waters now and no Mum, no Joan Waters left. Nobody, nothing but her.

Joan started a feud at dinner with the cashier. The menu was written on a blackboard by the door, each dish priced in yuan. She ordered crispy chicken, a vegetable dish, beef and rice and offered RMB notes.

The girl would not touch them. 'FEC,' she said stolidly.

Leah shrank a little, FEC, tourist money, meant they were now to pay double for the meal, and Joan wouldn't like it.

'Why? I'm eating the same food as everyone else, aren't I?'

'RMB is only for Chinese people.'

'I am Chinese.'

'You are Overseas Chinese. It is not the same.'

'That is not fair.'

'It is the rule.'

Joan lifted a finger, but sighed in defeat. 'All right.' She counted out the FEC notes calculated from the blackboard.

The girl still shook her head. She wrote down the figures from the blackboard – and doubled them.

'What?' Joan shouted at the girl.

'Tourists pay more. It is the rule.'

'You know what you can do with your meal!' Joan thrust Leah from the restaurant.

Joan and Leah ate below in the chaotic din of the third class restaurant. The food was barely tolerable, but, she paid for it with RMB and there was a gleam of triumph in her eye.

She had found another grey woman and this time she was not going to get kicked around.

The riverboat dropped an anchor briefly in Nanjing, a city of tall new buildings and a cluttered waterfront built on the ruins of massive imperial walls.

'Not the same as Good Field,' Joan said quietly.

'It's bigger.'

'The Japanese troops left the village alone. Here 300,000 people were killed.'

Joan was brooding over the city until a sudden red blaze of students disturbed her. 'Not again!'

'There's a lot of them.'

'Nothing new. In 1976 they painted slogans on a train, attacking Mao's Cultural Revolution. Students in Beijing read the slogans when the train arrived and took over Tiananmen Square. That almost finished the Decade of Chaos.'

'Is that happening now?'

'Now? No, just kids mucking about. No, not now.' Joan was persuading herself

Leah spent hours on the riverboat's foredeck, watching lush green and yellow plains sliding slowly past. Through the trees lining the river she could see an occasional bullock ploughing a paddy, women planting rice seedlings, a distant village. She half-dozed under a hazy sun, stroking the peg doll and wondering what Swallow was doing now.

'Now there's something the Chinese are doing right!' Joan bounced to the rail beside Leah and pointed.

Leah saw the brown water and the flat bank, nothing else.

'The trees, the trees! Look at them, they're everywhere.'

Young trees, carefully planted and tended. She had seen them at Good Field, on hills outside the train to Shanghai, now they were crowding the sides of the Yangtze, around a village, on the edge of a road.

Leah hunched her back. 'So?'

'They're fixing up the country after Mao's back-yard furnaces. The greening of China.'

The coughing man erupted and spat heavily into the river.

Leah looked rigidly ahead.

'Are you enjoying this, Leah?'

'Sure. Why?'

Joan rubbed her knuckles on the rail. 'Because you don't seem to like China one bit. I thought we were getting on very well when we left Good Field, but now . . .'

'What do you expect when you beat me about the head?'

'How long are we going to go on about that? All right, I was in the wrong. I should not have done it. But can we move on?'

Leah stared rigidly at the river. 'There's more. There's been more ever since Dad died and you rushed us into China.'

'It's not like that . . .' The coughing man moved toward them. 'We had better talk. Later.'

'Later' became much later. Joan wandered about the boat by herself as the river became a chain of lakes: calm brown water with patches of mysterious darker brown.

Leah watched smaller boats slowly replace coastal freighters, and her comfortable anger began to curdle into guilt. She shook the feeling by bouncing her memory into the time before. Before the Cough, before the coin, before everything.

That was when Dad brewed his own beer and one day twenty two bottles exploded in the laundry, the cat took off for a week and Mum kept telling him he was lucky she didn't know any ancient Chinese curses, because otherwise . . . That was when Dad and Mum sang Danny Boy for a holiday party and it was so horrible they were disowned by their beloved daughter. That was when said daughter started a car-wash business and Dad wound up re-washing cars to keep the owners happy. That was also the time the beloved daughter came wailing home because some of the boys called her a 'Chink'. She wasn't, was she? Dad, not Mum, filled her six-year-old mind with the glories of the emperors, the ancient inventions, the navigators. So much that she was an Empress for two weeks. Come to think of it, that was the first time she had seriously considered Mum was Chinese.

Leah was smiling as the riverboat slid up to a flat barge, old, with a shack thrown up near the stern. The barge was steered by a small boy. He saw Leah and waved.

Leah was waving back as Joan joined her warily. 'Lucky,' said Leah.

'C'mon for lunch. She surrendered.'

'Oh. The restaurant lady?'

'Yup. We started a mutiny. Other tourist passengers were going to join us in third class, or go hungry. We pay FEC, but only what the blackboard says. Victory! Who's lucky?'

'That boy there. Huckleberry Finn.'

Joan shook her head. 'Goes up and down the Yangtze with his family, lives on the river, but he probably never gets any education.'

'That's lucky.' Leah stopped. 'All his life on the river.'

'Yes. He can't do anything else, can he? Lucky? C'mon.'

Suddenly the first voyage was over. They stepped onto the windy streets of Wuhan, deep in the

central plain of China, half way between Guangzhou in the south and Beijing in the north. They
stopped to watch a passionate old man on a crate
shouting at a stirring crowd of riverside workers.
Two youths were painting a message on a red
banner behind him.

'It is not just the students,' Joan said softly.

'What is it?' Something big was happening.

'I don't know. But it's the same as Nanjing, as
Shanghai, as Tiananmen Square in Beijing.'

Leah could hear the anxiety in Joan's voice. They
were in the middle of China. They might not get
out.

But Wuhan had no disturbances that day. Joan
had to battle through the usual crowd for tickets
upriver, but they then found an old colonial hotel
with high ceilings, stained walls and a chandelier
in the lobby, and unfolded for a rest. They walked
the quiet streets that night in search of a restaurant.
But it was nine o'clock and the river city had gone
to sleep. They ordered noodles at a workers' café.

Joan put the coin on the table and leaned back.
'Now we talk.'

Leah locked her eyes on the coin and fished for
her old anger.

'I didn't know how you felt about China. I
thought the trip and the coin were as important to
you as they were to me. Maybe more . . .'

'You were so fast – the day after the funeral you
were talking about studying for China. Getting
ready for the trip. The day after!'

'Don't you see? No, you don't see. You haven't
had the night of the mob. You must try to
understand.'

Joan turned the coin with a finger. 'I was eight
years old when they came. A terrible yammering
in the air, I'll never forget the sound. Father looked
down the street and there was a tide of men with

75

machetes, clubs and torches. Mother rushed me off the street and Father started to close the shutters. Then he changed his mind and got us out of the shop, running very hard down the street.

'The mob were breaking windows, tearing the shutters from the shop of a neighbour, Ah Fang, throwing torches inside. Ah Fang hobbled to the door and tried to run away but the men with the machetes . . . Mother covered my eyes, but I *know* what happened.'

For an instant Leah saw that night through the eyes of a very little girl. Terrible! So terrible the little girl could never forget it, seeing it on a TV screen in Guangzhou, in a train, in a lane in Shanghai.

But what did that have to do with Dad? 'Why were the men angry?' Leah asked the question quickly, to give herself time to think.

Joan made a sound almost like laughter. 'They were a mob. A mob does not need a reason. Like the Japanese in Janjing, like the soldiers in Shanghai. In Penang they were Malays, we were Chinese. That was reason enough.

'So the fire spread from Ah Fang's shop to ours, and that was the end. We left for Singapore three days later. You understand?'

Leah looked blankly at Joan.

'No you don't. The night of the mob taught me something important. When everything's gone, when there's nothing more you can do, it is best to turn away. Change things, go somewhere else. When Father phoned me in Sydney to tell me Mother had died I took a bus to northern Queensland. Father stayed home in Singapore but he painted the family flat. We knew what to do.'

'So we came to China to forget about Dad,' Leah said bluntly. 'I don't want to forget him. Ever.'

'You aren't understanding.' Joan rose unsteadily

to her feet and touched Leah's hand. 'We're tired. Look after the coin.'

They returned to the hotel, their steps echoing in the empty street.

10 Gorges

The second riverboat was much the same as the first boat, single funnel with red star, a lounge for the second class passengers, two restaurants, airy comfort near the bridge, packed bodies and air reeking with tobacco smoke everywhere else. They were allotted an inside cabin but they would spend nearly all their time on deck. A few steps away there were showers, but one shower seemed to be on all the time.

The boat yawed into the river current, dodged a hooting cross-river ferry, passed under a massive bridge and left Wuhan behind. No more freighters now, but smaller, flatter barges sitting on flat lazy water, and fishing boats drifting with the current. Lone hills occasionally broke the monotony of the flat plain.

Joan left Leah alone on deck and read a book. Leah rubbed the coin with her thumb as she leant on the rail.

We are still chasing the coin, Dad, but it is getting so complicated. Oh, *I'm* not complicated. I'm still after what you wanted, the mystery of the coin, but who knows what Joan wants? When you were here, she wanted to follow her father's last request – to take the coin to his ancestral village, right? But when you were gone she wanted to find the only family she had in the world, fast, and to forget about you. Then in Good Field it was her father's request, again, and now it's all about forgetting you – again.

Leah held the coin over the brown river.

The coin was the end of the fun days. Wish it had never come. Oh, there were good times afterward, even after the Cough began, but there was always a little bit of cloud hanging about. The arrival of the coin was the first time – and just about the last time – she had seen Joan crying.

A sudden string of explosions jerked Leah's head up as the side of a hill slid down into a rising fog of brown dust.

Startled, she clutched the coin, pulled it back from the river. She opened her hand slowly and stroked the black metal. She was frowning, as if it had somehow changed.

There was nothing to watch in the port of Yichan except for the captain's docking procedure. So Leah stood with Joan in the long light of the setting sun and supervised. The riverboat had slowed fifty metres out from a small stretch of vacant dock and was moving up against the heavy current.

'Lovely to see a man doing what he knows,' Joan said. 'Even out here. Especially out here.'

The bow anchor was let go with a running rattle and the engine slowed down.

Leah looked at Joan. Was she thinking of her father?

'Watch him. He's going to make the river work for him.'

Once Joan would talk about her old man, a mechanic with magic fingers. Motorbikes, diesel tractors, sewing machines, anything he touched he fixed. He was learning computers near the end.

She could talk about him making a windmill drive a motor carcase as a pump, and she even sounded as if she understood it all.

The boat was drifting slowly backwards and sideways.

But she never talked about him now.

The anchor chain was clanking off the boat, link by link.

But everything happened so fast. She'd be talking about him, then the letter and the coin arrived, then the house went empty and quiet, then Dad started pushing toward China, then the Cough.

'He hardly needs the engines now . . .'

The riverboat's bow cleared the stern of the ferry on the dock.

Then the verdict and Joan wasn't crying this time.

A line thrown casually from the bow to two men wearing gloves on the dock. The line caught and pulled, dragging the heavy cable from the boat.

All this in a month! Four lousy weeks.

The cable was over the bollard and the boat's winch tightened the cable, pulling the bow toward the wharf. The stern swung in to the wharf, the stern cable was secured and the stern winch began to grind.

'Oh, he's good. I want to clap,' Joan said.

The boat snuggled between the other boats, nudged the wharf and stopped. There was no room left even for a rowboat.

Leah followed Joan inside, dead faced, to be stopped by a small pandemonium. The ever-running shower had burst and was gushing water out of its cubicle. Two drenched youths wrestled with the shower, armed with a very large monkey-wrench, while two girls desperately mopped the sodden carpet.

'See,' beamed Joan. 'It's the same the world over. We old coots can do it, you kids haven't a clue.'

Next morning the riverboat pulled itself out to the anchor and shouldered into the Yangtze. A little later the riverboat reached a high concrete wall stretching across the Yangtze, pouring brown water from multiple turrets to feed the river.

'Gezhouba Dam,' Joan said, and she sounded impressed. 'We're catching a lift.'

'It's huge,' said Leah. She watched two massive metal doors slowly open ahead. Another riverboat and a barge scuttled out like cockroaches.

The boat nudged forward through the scarred doors, with Leah leaning back, looking up at the top of the lock. A mouse in a dungeon. Hydraulic rams, thick as funnels, began to close the doors very slowly.

Leah felt a sudden impact, solid as a blow.

It had been like this!

After Dad's news, nothing ended. Not at first. Dad went out and sold cars, Mum tended plants at the nursery, and she went to school. Everything was the same, like the broad brown river at the stern of the boat, but there was a great dark door slowly closing.

Mum pushed her out with Dad, so they could go bushwalking, down the ancient Aboriginal path to the shining water of their secret cove. Watch gulls wheel over Lion Island, a schooner set rust-red sails for the Marquesas Islands. But then it became too far to walk. They drove to the Ku-ring-gai headland, the three of them, and picnicked with the crowd. 'What fun!' said Mum, and it was for a bit. Then Dad stopped selling cars and stayed home and read.

Leah stared intensely at the steadily reducing slit

between the two doors, seeing only the last of the sunlit river.

Bald now, and walking on a stick – but he often reversed it and putted pebbles out of the way. He took the family to the movies, until he had to stay in the toilet for half an hour with the Cough.

The doors hissed together, leaving the riverboat in hazy shadows. Water began to thunder into the bottom of the lock.

In hospital, out of hospital. Shrinking. But always trying to laugh. Home in bed with so many pills and medicines, out of bed in a wheel chair. Playing chess in the sun, with frangipani blossoms falling on the board. Daughter winning, should not be winning.

The riverboat began to rise.

In bed all the time. Mum at home, playing cards with Dad when he was awake, cleaning things when he wasn't. She moved into your bedroom and set up a bunk, because she was afraid of hurting him. Became 'Joan'.

Leah was caught by the sunlight slanting over the metal wall and closed her eyes.

Just a shadow now, melting away. Wouldn't see anyone. Eyes staring from a waiting skull.

The thundering water slowed, and stopped.

Joan picked you up from school half way through the morning. She said, 'He's gone.'

The doors off the boat's bow – just booms lying on the river now – began to open.

Then the funeral and you couldn't stop thinking, 'It's over. Thank God it's over.' No matter how hard you tried.

And you were angry with Joan!

As the riverboat moved into the upper Yangtze Joan clicked her tongue. 'Well, how did you like that ride?'

'It's over.' Leah took Joan's hand and squeezed. 'We've been through a lot, eh?'

'Ah, yes.' Joan looked at her with a slight touch of puzzlement.

The gorges started almost immediately. Hills became mountains and slid together, squeezing the broad, slow Yangtze into a narrow surge.

We've left the flat land, Leah thought. Down there is Good Field and Swallow and Grandfather. Up here are the mountains, Turtle Land and the secret of the coin. Let's get on with it!

Tiny villages clung to high ridges with terraces etched desperately far above them. The sun swam feebly in a pass thick with mist. The beat of the boat was echoed in the constant crash of toppling waterfalls. A mountain ahead had been cleft cleanly to let the river twist through. Tiny boats rode the river downstream as if they were surfing, as tiny boats fought the river upstream in exhausted gasps along the rock walls, eddy by eddy. Five men hurled a rowboat against the current, flailing the water furiously with their oars.

The riverboat cut across a calm stretch, nearing a small valley of moss-streaked boulders and sheltered pines. And a pure blue river. The blue of the mountain water met the brown of the Yangtze, pushed it back, flowed with it for a few metres, cutting a clean line between the blue and the brown. Then the Yangtze humped over a rock and there was no more blue.

Joan hunched over the rail, looking back. 'He should have seen that.'

Leah blinked at Joan, and nodded. 'Yeah.' She was smiling.

A little later the gorge opened up and a coal town squatted among the green banks and the grey mountains. A battery of chimneys pumped smoke across the river, ramshackle buildings seemed to be slowly collapsing. Trucks tipped coal down the river bank adding to the spreading fans of fine black. Long chains of men and women carried baskets of coal on their shoulders from the piles to a waiting fleet of barges, and trudged back for more.

The riverboat twisted round a bend and the stepped forests and waterfalls of the gorges returned. But that little town was a taste of the giant at the end of the run.

11 Fortress

All morning the boat had wound through black hills under a sky heavy with smoke. A fuming factory sat on every ridge. Every metre of muddy slope was covered with a shell of rickety grey shacks. If there had ever been a splash of colour on those slopes, the smoke and the rain had long since washed it away. There were no trees, no bushes living in the acid-tasting air.

'Chongqing,' said Joan. 'The last bastion.'

Leah shivered. She knew Chiang Kai-shek's troops had retreated before the Japanese armies from Shanghai, from Nanjing, from Wuhan, to here. Here they stayed. Nearly every night Japanese bombers followed the gleam of the Yangtze to unload on yesterday's fires. The last bomb had fallen forty-five years ago, but Leah could not shake the feeling that the war had not stopped. Chongqing was still an embattled fortress.

The boat nudged a floating wharf at the foot of a long, long climb of greasy steps and stopped.

'Here we go, stick with me.' Joan swung her suitcase out of the cabin.

A man helped Joan with her suitcase past the beginning of the steps and left her near an inclining cable car before she could thank him. They slid past the staggering steps and the blackened buildings to a high road, where they caught a taxi.

It's getting better, Leah thought. A bit.

'Renmin Hotel,' Joan ordered. She smiled at Leah. 'A people's palace, built in the 1950s. We deserve that for a day.'

The taxi climbed above the slate grey slums and to a broad gate at the top of a hill. Behind the gate was an expanse of lawn and a great curved red and gold building, an emperor's dream. But the steps were blocked by banners and a swelling crowd, and the gate was sealed by a body of white-capped police. The taxi driver was waved away.

'Bloody students!' Joan muttered. 'They've taken over the hotel.'

The taxi driver drove on, looking for another hotel.

Joan frowned. 'I don't understand. The police still aren't doing anything.'

They found a hotel in the heart of town, bought train tickets for Chengdu for tomorrow and Joan decided that she needed a good bath followed by a long nap.

'And you? Going to read a book, or something?'

Leah shuffled about a bit. 'Ah, d'you mind if I walk around?'

'Here? In this place?' Joan's face tightened.

Leah looked away. They were both remembering Shanghai. 'I won't go far. I won't get lost.'

'You don't know what it's like out there – the students – it may be danger – ' Joan stopped and closed her eyes. 'Doing it again, aren't I? Seeing the mob everywhere we go. Must stop that. All right, go – but be careful.'

Leah strode out of the hotel, but she took with her the glimpse of Joan's face, eyes heavy with anxiety. She almost went back. She had only been testing the water, seeing if Joan had changed since Shanghai, but Joan was now letting her go, completely. She did not know if she wanted all that freedom.

Oh, come on, you can't stop now.

Leah turned a corner and walked into a march of protesting students. She raised her camera, but a spectator shook his head and waved her down.

You're in the heart of China. Things are happening. Just look.

She left the students and wandered along sooty streets, snapping as she went. She saw there were very few bicycles on the streets and was able to work out the reason: hills made for goats. She wandered through a covered food market, hanging meat, black bananas, small oranges, blotched cabbage. Bad fruit and vegetables because the soil was being poisoned by Chongqing's factories. She skirted a few police with walkie-talkies.

She stopped to watch a pavement 'doctor' treat a woman by attaching minerals to her ear, and a crowd gathered to watch her. She was moving on when the doctor saw her.

'The ear is the key to the body. You know that?' He spoke in heavily accented putonghua, and Leah battled to understand.

'I didn't know.'

'Anything, arthritis, constipation, lung infection, they can be treated through the ear. You have something wrong?'

'No, thank you.'

'You are from America. You see the students?'

'Australia. Yes, before.'

'They are foolish. They cannot remember the bad years.'

'The Decade of Chaos? The Red Guards?'

'And before. When Chiang Kai-shek was here. When the bombs were falling. Chiang's secret police were throwing students into prison. Chiang, Red Guards, it does not matter. *Now* is a dangerous time.'

Leah said goodbye to the ear doctor and walked downhill. She saw a crowd around an intersection and stopped to adjust her camera.

A youth suddenly pointed at her camera and called to her and she looked up in alarm.

But the youth only wanted her to go up a pedestrian overpass. She did what she was told and joined a small crowd looking down on an empty road. A young woman with a camera made room for Leah and hers. There were police on the overpass and along the road.

'What is happening?' Leah said.

The young woman frowned as she battled through Leah's putonghua. 'Ah, yes, Beijing,' she said in English. 'Look.'

Leah could see the swirl and billow of red flags and banners above the slope of grey slums. She could even hear the rapid beat of a single drum.

'The government has still not promised to change things . . .'

Hundreds of spectators pressed against the traffic barriers and a roar swept the road like surf. People were clapping around the police, some younger men making slow fists as the march reached them. The woman leaned over the rail and worked her camera under the impassive gaze of a policeman five metres away. The drum passed below Leah, beaten with style and a little pomp by a girl with four straining men taking the weight. Leah smiled nervously at the policeman, but she took photos. The drum team grinned up at her and held up quick Victory signs. The road was filled with marchers and banners as far as Leah could see.

The woman with the camera yelled over the noise at Leah. 'In Beijing, in Tiananmen Square, one thousand students have gone on a hunger strike. Until the government moves.'

Leah stared at the girl with the drum and for a final moment the girl with the drum stared at her.

She looks like me, Leah thought in surprise. The same size as me, the same smile as me. She can only be two years older than me.

I could be her.

12 Search

On the train Leah told Joan what she had seen and heard the day before: how the students had tramped in their thousands beneath her feet, how a woman with a camera kept telling her about things that were happening in Tiananmen Square as if it was just round the corner, how the students started a hunger strike and party boss Zhao Ziyang came out of the Politburo and pleaded with the students to go home. They wouldn't, and today Russia's Gorbachev would visit Beijing – and that would embarrass Boss Deng no end . . .

Leah was taking a furtive delight in rolling the strange names off her tongue.

Joan heard all this with a frown. 'At least they

87

have planes running straight from Chengdu to Hong Kong. We can leave.'

But the students were forgotten when the train stopped with a clang and a hiss in Chengdu. For the next couple of days they rushed about the ancient and exotic city like tourists on a package tour. They found a quiet hotel near a bus terminal and the muddy Nanhe River. They tried very, very hot Sichuanese cooking which left them both in tears – and laughing. They walked from modern buildings to the preserved home of ancient poet Du Fu, and temples. They wandered along streets lined with trees, found markets winding down shady lanes, discovered women from Tibet selling craftwork . . .

Leah felt things were changing. Joan was enjoying herself and beginning to relax. She wore a garish mandarin hat for an entire morning just for the hell of it, and allowed Leah to lead her through a dark alley with no more than a mutter about 'killer's corner'.

It was funny, Leah thought, how things changed every time they moved. In Guangzhou Joan was a stranger, on the first train she was an ally, in Shanghai an enemy, in Wuhan a little girl with a nightmare, in Chongquin a mother. And in Chengdu, somehow, they had become sisters again. For a short time they both forgot about the coin . . . until Leah saw an old medallion in a footpath stall and pulled the coin from her purse to compare them.

Joan saw the coin in her hand. 'Oh, yes. Holiday's over, let's find this little beast.'

The sallow woman looked down her nose at Joan and shook her head. 'There is no village of that name anywhere near Chengdu.'

'But you haven't even looked.'

'I do not need to look. Gui Tu Cun, Turtle Land Village. That is a name from the days of the emperors. Decadent. If such a village still exists, it has a new name, a far finer name.'

'Oh. But you must have a record of the new name.'

'We have records of everything. Of every village in Sichuan . . .'

'Then you must be able to tell me what Turtle Land is called now, and where it is.'

'I cannot.'

'Why?'

'The name was probably changed in 1949 when the People's Republic of China was born. It is a long time ago.'

'Can't you look back?'

'No. I have no time.'

Joan's fingers went white on the counter. 'Can *I* look?'

'No foreigner is allowed in our file room. Good day.'

Leah pulled Joan away from the counter quickly before she lost her temper.

They returned to the neighbourhood of their hotel and brooded at an open café table at the edge of the city canal. They sucked bottles of yoghurt through thick straws but Joan was not drinking the yoghurt, she was attacking it.

'What do we do now?' Leah said.

'I'd like to go back and strangle that woman.' Joan was demolishing a castle of yoghurt in her squat bottle. 'She was not only not helping us – she was obstructing us.'

'Perhaps she thought you were a spy.'

Joan snorted. 'Well, I don't know what to do. Go back to the China Travel Service and get pointed in another direction. We can't just go out in the country and hope to blunder across the village.'

'Might as well, though . . .'

They looked bleakly at the empty bottles.

The café owner came over with worry shadowing his face. 'There is something wrong? Bad yoghurt?' He stumbled over his English.

'No, no, this is lovely.' Joan flicked a smile at the man.

'We were just thinking of ways of finding a village, that's all.'

'Your village?'

'We think so. Our ancestral village.'

'Ah.' He shook Joan's hand vigorously and hauled up a vacant chair. 'Welcome back. What is the name of your village?'

'Gui Tu.'

'Turtle Land. That is the old name. You don't have the new one?'

'No. That's our trouble.'

'Turtle Land. Turtle Land . . . Maybe your village is in the direction of Guan Xian. Many records were lost in the Decade of Chaos but old people remember. There is a story about a turtle-god giving water to farmers in the dry lands. And the story comes from a very old irrigation project at Guan Xian.'

Leah balanced on the balls of her feet and tried to see a snowy peak beyond the brown hills on the horizon. Nothing, but she was seeing the end of the great Red Plain and westward those hills would stack like cards into the Himalayas. She was almost seeing Tibet.

The old man they had met thought about Gui Tu for a while, as he turned from the distant barrier of the hills. 'That is an old, old name. We don't think of those days any more. Maybe you ask further south along the Min River.'

Joan and Leah moved west to the old and new works of the Dujiangyan Irrigation Project at Guan Xian.

Two thousand three hundred years ago, when the Great Wall of China was just beginning to be built, the governor of the kingdom of Sui, Li Ping, dug channels to stop the Min river from thundering over villages and fields every time the snow melted. And a canal was cut through a mountain to turn a barren plain into rich farmland. Li Ping and his son were called kings after their deaths and the ruler of that part of China, Emperor Chong, became a Turtle God.

But there was no sign of Turtle Land village.

They turned wearily from Guan Xian and followed the Min River back toward Chengdu.

'Turtle Land? No, we were Golden Land, after the wheat, I think. No, never heard of it.'

'There was a Turtle village just north of the river junction. I don't think it was Turtle Land, though.'

'No, we were Turtle Egg. It is a pity.'

'No, cannot help. Maybe it does not exist now. After 1949 villages became communes and some little villages were destroyed.'

The old woman stopped shelling her peas and squinted at the lowering sun. 'Just you wait . . . my memory hurts . . .'

Leah scratched her leg with her other foot and Joan sagged a little more.

The old woman finally shrugged in defeat. 'I am

sorry, I don't know. It is so long ago. Before the Decade of Chaos, before Chairman Mao visited us, before the famine, before the making of communes. All those years . . .'

'That's all right. Thank you for trying.' Joan turned toward the quietly steaming taxi.

'There is Red Star village, just down the road. It had a fish, or turtle name, but I cannot remember.'

'Thank you.' Joan smiled weakly as she walked away. 'Come on Leah, I've had it. We're going home.'

13 Red Star

Leah trailed after Joan, weary from the weight of many disappointments. She could not even muster the strength to try for one last try. She had felt the fire of Dad's enthusiasm at home, in Good Field, even in the shadows of Shanghai and in the long days on the river, but here there was nothing but shaking heads, wrong roads and cold villages. She had done her best, but now there was nothing left. It was time to go home.

Joan stopped in the centre of the track. The bonnet of the taxi was up, steam was drifting lazily from deep in the engine well, the feet of the driver were sticking out from beneath the car.

'Oh no,' she sighed and tapped the man's shoe with her foot. 'Trouble?'

The driver skewed his head clear. He looked greasy and unhappy. 'Water hose . . .' He exploded his fingers apart.

'When will you fix it?'

'Half hour – hour.' He shrugged, and slid back under the taxi.

'We are going home. Definitely,' Joan turned angrily from the taxi.

Leah nodded. She had never felt so much in agreement with Joan as now. 'But what do we do now?'

'Wait. What else is there to do?'

'We could walk over to this Red Star village.' The final flicker. Leah was surprised by the words as she said them.

'What's the point . . .?' Then Joan may have thought of her father's final wish, or she may simply have noticed the curious crowd gathering around her. 'Oh, come on,' she said.

The gravel track wound back to the highway and the highway lay across the plain, a featureless black slash running to the horizon. There were several other tracks leading from the highway to houses, to fields, to villages out of sight, to the coiling path of the Min River. Joan stopped on the highway, undecided.

A truck barrelled up the highway, and slowed as it approached them. Leah could see a forest of heads and a few poles with white and red cotton rolled round their ends, like broad bandages. A man slapped the cabin roof and the truck accelerated, leaving Leah blinking in the dust.

But the truck had left a single passenger beside the road, a young man with floppy hair and spectacles bandaged together. He was carrying a red flag, slapping it from one hand to the other while he played a silent rhythm with his lips and shuffled in the dust. He saw Leah and Joan and let his beat wind down, and grinned at them.

'You are looking for something?' he said in putonghua.

'Red Star village?' Leah tried.

He squinted at both Leah and Joan, trying to work out something. 'Yes,' he said in English. 'I live there. It is down there.' He pointed at the track behind him. 'I will show you.'

Joan hesitated, but Leah crossed the highway to the youth's side, forcing her to follow.

'You have someone to visit?' The youth ambled between small fields of sighing wheat.

'Perhaps, we don't know yet.'

'Is this Turtle Land village?' Joan said roughly.

The youth cocked his head. 'No, it is Red Star village.'

'Mum means in the olden days.'

'Mum? Oh, you are family. You are looking for family. I understand. My uncle, he is a teacher and knows about these things. He will be there now. Where are you from?'

They introduced each other as they walked, the youth shortening his name to 'Ke' to make things easier for fumble-tongued Leah. Some of the fields had been cut to stubble and a few women were walking ahead of them with a haystack on their shoulders and a sickle in their hands. They were approaching a broad copse of tall bamboo, a green eruption in a sea of rippling gold.

'You are a student, Ke?' Leah said, nodding at the rolled flag.

Ke grinned, flicked it open and flourished it. 'Not at the moment. We are on strike.'

'You are a protest marcher?' Joan frowned.

'In Chengdu. Hundreds of us, stopping the traffic.'

'That must be fun,' said Joan. 'Better than study.'

Ke looked sideways at Joan and his smile faded, then flashed back. 'Ah, yes, it's a great party!'

'Where's the village?' Joan sounded irritated.

94

'There, in the bamboo. The bamboo protects us from the sun and the wind.'

Leah could just see the low dark shape of houses through the bamboo. No double storeys, no Hong Kong houses, but that bamboo could have come from Good Field village.

Ke flapped his flag about. He was smiling at Joan but the flag was slashing the air, as if in anger.

'I heard of a thousand students on hunger strike in Beijing . . .' Leah said, to offset Joan's bite.

The flag slowed. 'In Tiananmen. But now it is three thousand. Sometimes it is not much of a party.'

They walked through the screen of bamboo and saw the village. Low wood and brick houses with small windows, no glass, old thatched roofs. A small brown dog barking at the intruders, a man thrashing wheat stalks with a wooden weight on the end of a long pole. A woman pumping water from a well.

'I knew it,' Joan said.

'It's great!'

'It's an old, old village.'

'It hasn't changed.'

'This is good?'

Ke frowned at Joan and led her toward a loud clanging sound. Five men behind a wall were making an axle spring for an almost finished trailer. Across from the mini-factory a group of men were sitting round tables, sipping rice spirit from small glasses and watching a black-and-white television. Ke moved toward a big man leaning his chair against a wall to catch the last streak of sun.

'Uncle,' said Ke quickly, 'these people are looking for their family. Can we help?'

The big man slowly opened an eye and he carried on conversation even more slowly as Ke pulled up some chairs. Leah could not believe that he was a teacher.

'So before you look for your family you must find the village?' said Uncle Tong.

'Yes please, Mr Tong,' Leah said.

'And you know it only by its imperial name.'

'Yes.'

'So you want to know this village's old name.'

Joan was fiddling.

'This village is now called Red Star.'

Leah looked at Joan. Will he never get round to it?

'But this village is old. Far older than the People's Republic. But it was one of the first villages to become a commune. Chairman Mao visited here once. And one of the last to stop being a commune. Oy! Quan! Will you stop that blasted hammering! I'm sure it was quieter when it was a commune.'

Get on with it!

'But it is old. Two thousand years. That's why it was called Turtle Land . . .'

Just like that. Leah was staring at Joan, a little uncertain that she had heard the words. But Joan was nodding.

'That what you wanted?'

'Oh yes, yes, yes!' Leah blurted it in English but Tong seemed to understand.

Suddenly they were on top of the world. Suddenly the terrors, the long journeys, the noisy hotels, the dirty restaurants were worth it. Suddenly Joan had found her father's ancestral village and *she* had found the home of the coin. Now for the story!

'Yes, that's the name we were after.' Joan was so calm.

'Now the family?'

The men had turned from the television to the teacher and the foreigners.

'Ji,' Joan said.

Tong frowned and glanced across at Ke.

'Means Pearl,' Leah tried.

Tong sighed. 'We do not know that name, Joan Waters.'

They cannot take it back now, Leah thought desperately. Not now. 'My mother's real name is Ji Feng Hua,' Leah said quickly.

Tong opened his hands in defeat.

'The coin, the coin . . .' Leah groped in her purse and held out the half coin.

Tong held it up to the last fading shaft of sunlight. Joan told the story of the broken coin quickly and waited. If she was feeling any tension she kept it from her face.

Tong stroked his cheek as he turned the half-coin. 'I am a teacher, but I am also a collector of coins. In my house I have a coin that is fifteen hundred years old. One finds coins here, in the earth, or when one digs a well. If someone finds a coin he brings it to me. If I can afford it I will buy it, if I cannot I can tell the finder how much it is worth.'

Tong looked from Joan to Leah and back again. 'But this coin – this strange piece of metal – I do not know this coin. And I do not know its story. I am sorry.'

Joan took the coin back with a shrug. 'Well, that is it . . .'

'Perhaps some family in the village might remember it?' Leah said feebly. This was not fair!

Tong spread his hands and shouted over a suddenly rising roar. 'There are very few secrets in Red Star. You could try – '

Joan kicked back her chair and twisted to her feet in alarm. 'The taxi! He'll never find us! Excuse . . .'

She weaved through the clustered men and darted round the corner of the café.

The roar became a squeal, a shout, a cry, a solid thump, and a skidding crash. A cloud of dust curled past the corner.

14 Accident

Leah swept her chair aside and ran to the corner, past slow-moving men and toppled chairs. Through the dust she could see the wall of the trailer factory and the bamboo, stark against the darkening sky. Beyond the bamboo and the wheat and the winding track, there may have been the taxi, searching. But it did not matter now.

Joan was sprawled in the dust with a motor-cycle lying on her back. A plump man in a grey suit was sitting on the ground adjusting his spectacles. Joan was absolutely still.

For a moment Leah stood rigid, choking, her fists banging against her legs. She started to run for the bike, clawing at the air and shouting.

Her arm was caught, swinging her wide, away from her mother. Ke was pulling at her, stepping in front of her, saying 'Wait' with his lips. Something in his eyes. He let her arm go and patted the air between them as he backed toward the bike. She could hear her breath thundering in her throat.

Ke moved slowly to the bike with Tong and two other men as the plump man began shouting angrily.

'Quiet, Heng.' Tong gripped the bike and waited

for the others to place themselves. He nodded and they lifted the bike straight up, walked sideways and bounced the bike back on its wheels.

'Mum . . .' Leah ducked to Joan's head.

Joan seemed to be flattening, becoming part of the earth, but dust particles were dancing before her nose. She was breathing. Tong passed his hand before her face, feeling the breath, lifted her dress slightly, ran his fingers down her spine gently and moved her upper leg. He said some words Leah did not understand.

'Concussion,' said Ke, to Leah. 'Exhaust burn on the leg, and Tong thinks there is a broken ankle . . .'

The plump man, Heng, started to shout again. Slower, and this time Leah could just about work out what he was saying. 'Look what this woman has done! Look, look!' He was wobbling a warped mudguard, but he was ignored.

'Get a stretcher, Ke,' said Tong.

'Rushed out on the road, just like that. Didn't look at all.'

'Xu Ping? How's the tractor? Yes, back here.'

'It wasn't my fault.'

Tong stood up. 'Going at that speed through the village . . . could've killed anyone.'

Heng stumbled a little and peered at Leah, then at Joan. 'Who are they?'

'Australians, looking for – '

'Foreigners! He looked at Joan as if she had bitten him.

Ke and another youth ran up with an army stretcher, shaking dust from it with every stride. It had been used many times, but not recently.

'What are you doing?'

'Taking this lady to hospital.'

Heng shook his head in a moment of alarm.

'No, no . . .' He was alarmed, fumbling. 'It's too far.'

'We're not going to Chengdu hospital.'

'Not Chengdu.' Suddenly Heng was almost smiling.

'The local hospital.'

'Yes, that is best. I will make arrangements.'

'They will probably send this lady on to Chengdu.'

'I will make arrangements.' Heng kicked his bike into life and rode away.

Ke watched him go. 'He's our village cadre. Our Party man. When I march I think of him.'

Joan was carefully eased onto the stretcher. The tractor, a long, low machine which rattled as it moved, arrived and one of the new trailers was hooked up. The stretcher carrying Joan was loaded onto the trailer and the tractor rocked slowly from the village.

Leah sat in the trailer and rubbed Joan's wrist. She had seen that being done on TV. 'Can't we go any faster?'

'Too rough,' Ke said. 'It'll be all right.'

The tractor turned away from the highway. It ran between two thin rows of trees, along an embankment beside a broad bend of the Min River, and up a slight hill. The hospital was an off-white building sheltered by a cluster of trees. Two men in white coats were waiting at the front.

Joan was carried along a cool corridor, past a cluttered dispensary, a washroom and toilet and into a three-bed room. It was empty. Leah was ushered out of the room by the white-coated men who had carried Joan, and a woman with a stethoscope went in.

'It's all right,' Ke said. 'She's good.'

Leah squeezed her hands together. She could not trust this flag-waving boy.

Ke led Leah to a small and simple lounge, and that also was empty. The hospital seemed almost deserted. Heng walked past the door, talking fast to a tall white-haired man, who nodded thoughtfully.

'Can you write your name?' Ke said suddenly.

'Of course.'

'I mean in Chinese.'

'Oh.' She did not feel like playing games. 'No.'

'That's a pity.'

'Yes.' She was listening for footsteps.

'What about your mother?'

'Yes. But she's next door, unconscious, isn't she?'

'She will be all right. Would she have written her Chinese name in Chinese on something in her bag?'

Leah glanced sharply at Ke, but she looked in the handbag on her lap. It was something to do. Passport, purse, address book, packet of aspirins, herbs from that grim Guangzhou market, lipstick, and the old letter written in thick black Chinese characters.

'No. Nothing. Mum knows Chinese to speak, but she doesn't know much about how to write it.' Where is that doctor?

'What about that letter?' Ke was looking over her shoulder.

'It's Grandad's. We can't really read it, but it's why we're here. That and the coin.' Leah looked up at the open door and rubbed her knuckles up her sleeve.

'Can I have a look?'

'Why?'

'I only want to see the signature.'

Leah picked up the letter, shrugged and handed it over.

Steps outside.

Ke began to unfold it very slowly.

Heng, the white-haired man and the woman doctor walked into the lounge. They were all smiling, but all differently: Heng, broadly, even triumphantly; the white-haired man, politely; the doctor, angry but smiling for Leah's benefit.

The woman doctor spoke first. 'Your mother is all right.'

Leah sagged and began to tremble. 'Can I see her now?' She was having trouble getting the words out.

The doctor opened her hand in regret. 'She is sleeping now. I have given her some tablets to reduce the pain. She is no longer suffering from concussion, but she does have a headache and has been mildly burned on her leg. She does have a fractured ankle. Normally, being a foreigner, she should be taken to Chengdu – '

'But this is not necessary,' the white-haired man said hurriedly. 'Your mother needs only some rest and this hospital can give her rest and care better than any Chengdu hospital. Mr Fan Heng has kindly made sure she will receive excellent food and comfort while she is here.'

Heng nodded and smiled with a glint of gold, and the woman doctor looked as if she was about to spit.

'And Mr Heng has offered the hospitality of his house to you while your mother recovers from this unfortunate accident.'

'Well . . .'

'It is not necessary,' said Ke. He was holding the letter and he was fighting down a grin. 'Leah should stay in my family's house. She is my family.'

15 Names

Back in the village Ke was showing the letter to Tong and to his mother, Li-Nan.

'You see? The name at the bottom? It's us!'

Tong took the letter from Ke and spread it before Li-Nan.

The woman smiled softly at Leah, as if she was sharing a secret joke.

'You understand, Leah?' said Ke.

Leah stared blankly at the letter.

'The name, your mother's name, Ji, it doesn't mean much. You can say it in so many ways, Jey, Jay, Jee, Zhiy and it can mean so many things: famine, engine, chicken, shoes, lucky, a book . . .'

Leah suddenly realized that she had stopped playing games with names. She could have worked out Ke was a visitor, Tong was a boy and Li-Nan was Experience-Child, but she hadn't. Ke was Ke and that was that – apart from when he was called Ah Ke by his mother, and 'Ah' didn't mean anything at all, just a way of calling the boy Ke with affection. Maybe she was beginning to think Chinese. But now the Chinese were playing games with names.

'For a start,' said Tong.

'But for every different meaning there is a special Chinese character,' said Ke, with a clap.

Ke spun the letter from under Tong's eyes and jabbed at it. Tong looked at Ke through the thatch of his eyebrows.

'Your mother says she is of the Ji family,' said Ke. 'But your grandfather does not write that. He writes something else.'

'We think,' said Tong.

Ke hesitated for a moment. 'That is Ji.' He picked up some paper and made some marks on it with a pen. 'That is your Ji – a pearl.' A ragged capital E and an even more ragged flag on a tripod. 'Now look at the letter.'

A ragged flag on a tripod. With a slash instead of the E.

He tapped the slash. 'That could be anything – a mistake copied for generations. Many people in China did not know how to write their names. Or maybe it is a sick man trying to write this.'

Ke scrawled a flag on a tripod with no E, no slash.

'Your family name?' Leah said softly.

Ke nodded. 'Zhu. Meaning the colour red.'

'They do look alike, don't they?' Leah said, standing on her excitement. She looked at Tong, and his face was bland.

'Very much,' said Ke.

'But we're Ji, not Zhu. We're Pearl, not Red.'

'Now. Now you are Cantonese, we are Sichuanese. We speak differently. A person who was a Zhu here a hundred years ago may have changed the sound of his name when he lived in Canton. He may have become a Zhao, a Jao, a Ji. And if he cannot write, the letter-writers and the officials may make his family Red, or Pearl as time goes by.'

'Can this be right?' Leah asked Tong.

'Oh yes, it is possible.'

'But you don't think so.'

Tong rubbed his hands. 'I don't know, Leah. You were looking for the Turtle Land village and this is Turtle Land. You were looking for your family and maybe we are. I just don't want to give you any false hopes.'

'And it doesn't matter.' Li-Nan firmly pushed Tong aside and placed her hand on Leah's forearm.

'You are in this house. You are part of our family now. Welcome.'

Leah looked at the angular woman with the fine laugh lines around her eyes and the wisps of grey in her swept-back hair, and wanted to hug her. There was something like understanding in her eyes, as if she had been hurt and saw it in others.

For a moment Leah felt that she was being pulled home.

'And it is better than staying at Heng's house,' said Ke.

16 Turtle Land

Leah stretched drowsily and felt the hard wood with her toe. For a minute she was still at home, waiting for the slow grind of a truck, the shriek of the kids next door. Then she heard the bray of angry geese and she was in China, in gentle Good Field village. But the bed was harder and different and far older. Ah yes, in Red Star village, no, in Turtle Land. Her family home – perhaps.

She wondered about that. The warm glow of Li-Nan's welcome was still there, and it had not been quite that way at Good Field. Swallow and Jade were closer, but they were sort of friends, like Rose and Ben at home. This was different.

Because she was not worried about the way Joan was thinking this time? Or perhaps *she* was changing, somehow. This time she really *wanted* to be part of the family. Now she had to find the missing part of the coin, both for Dad and for herself.

She slid out from under the warm quilted bed-cover and stepped onto the straw mat with a shiver. It was cold. She hopped about trying to get her feet into her socks under the glittering eyes of the dragons that crowned her two hundred year old bed. She stumbled and fell awkwardly to the packed earth floor.

'All right, Leah?' Li-Nan called from outside.

'Fine,' shouted Leah. 'Fine.' But that earth floor, trampled and swept every day for two thousand years, felt like concrete.

Ke greeted her in the kitchen with a kettle of hot water for her to wash herself, apologising for the din of the geese. And the ducks and the pigs. 'Sorry to wake you up. Sleep well?'

'Great, I'm getting used to ducks and geese, now.'

'Ah, yes, you've been in a Chinese village before. But maybe we're not the same.'

Leah looked outside. Four low, thatched build-ings formed the walls of a square courtyard and Li-Nan was feeding the geese on a low hump outside this courtyard. The walls of three of the buildings were stucco, with windows but no glass. The other building did not have any inner walls and was filled with hay and large woven baskets. There was a thick old tree in the centre of the courtyard, with a bicycle leaning against it and three wooden chairs facing the sun.

'A little older,' Leah tried.

'Ah, yes. Maybe too old. Maybe we should have houses with wooden floors and gas stoves, hey? And the animals and the birds, you see them?'

'They look very nice.'

'They ought to be! They get more food – much more – than in any ordinary village. I think they eat better than us.' Ke was smiling, but with a touch of annoyance in the smile.

'But why?'

Ke pointed at two sagging, almost empty bags in the corner of the storeroom. 'That's all the fertilizer we have left for the next harvest. The government only lets us have two bags instead of five, and that is the same all over the village. So we have to make our own fertilizer.'

'Lucky animals.'

'Pig heaven.'

Ke worked up the fire in the blackened concrete wok stove and prepared a breakfast of eggs and noodles while Li-Nan finished feeding the livestock. Tong strolled across the courtyard from his house and stayed for a few cups of tea before pedalling off to his school.

Li-Nan looked thoughtfully at her son. 'And you are still on strike?'

Ke looked sharply up at Leah. 'Until they surrender!' And he grinned.

'You think they ever will?' Li-Nan moved to clear the plates, smiling wearily, as though they had been through this many times before. Like an old dance.

'But today the battle will have to go on without me. Today I want to show Leah what she is part of.'

Li-Nan looked relieved. 'I will make a lunch. You must show Leah the way to the hospital.'

Ke stopped by the pig pen and snorted. The sow ignored the squealing piglets tumbling about her feet and nosed through the pile of vegetables and grain mash. She snorted back.

'Your turn will come,' Ke said sweetly. 'Crackling and sweet and sour sauce. Lovely.' He snapped his teeth together.

The sow hesitated a moment and stared up with

her black-button eyes before ploughing into a mound of slop.

'You shouldn't have done that,' Leah said. 'She heard it.'

'Good. Everybody should know where they stand . . .'

It's like running around with a little brother, Leah thought suddenly. He's what, eighteen, but he's only a clown.

Ke took Leah along a narrow path running between the houses and the fields as the Turtle Land village settled into its rhythm. Children wearing red scarves trailed from their thatched houses and followed Tong to school. An old woman heaved on a rusty pump to fill a bucket with water with a lazy dog sprawled at her feet. A tall man strode into the fields with a yoke of two buckets slopping manure. A youth was flailing at grain in a courtyard in combat, dancing back, kicking high as he brought the flail down with a whoop.

'Watch out for Deng!' Ke shouted.

The young man grunted and kicked back at a tree that was padded far above his head.

'Karate nut,' Ke said.

'Deng Xiaoping? I thought he was a hero.' Leah remembered Grandfather's sneer at students for criticising Deng.

'Was. Suppose he can still be. If he did the right thing. You know he's one of us? Came from Sichuan, but we're not proud of him now. Too worried about staying the boss of China.'

It's very hard to pick your heroes in China, Leah thought.

They walked past the hammering of the trailer factory, the whirr and dull thump of a very small rug factory and a repair shop.

'And this was one of Mao's favourite spots.

That's why the village was called Red Star. He visited us. So of course we were one of the first villages to become a commune in 1950 and one of the last to stop being a commune ten years ago . . . Ah, you aren't interested in Chinese politics.'

'I don't know much about the politics of *my* country, either.'

'Sure. Because they don't affect you. Here they affect all of us. Sorry, sorry, change the subject. We go and see your mother now, okay?'

Joan was lying on a bed that looked as hard as a park bench, alone in a room with one light, one window, no curtains. The walls were painted dark green to head height and then white. Joan was wearing a simple surgical gown and a plastic hospital bracelet. She was happy to see Leah, but she was weak.

'How do you feel, Mum?' Leah was just relieved to see Joan conscious.

'They are very nice to me here, dear. Nice food, peaceful . . .' She sounded like an old woman, her words resting on her breath.

'That's good. I'm living in the Turtle Land village, not far from here. And Ke has worked out from your father's signature – '

'Only I still hurt. In my leg and in my head.'

'The doctor says you are recovering very well.'

'Yes. I must get better. Sleep is the best thing.'

They walked away from the hospital, across the whispering plain of wheat and down to the brown river.

'Don't worry about it,' Ke said. 'She's just tired. Heng gave her body a terrible jerk.'

'I'm not worrying. Much.'

Ke looked sideways. 'You and your mother . . . You must be very close.'

Leah was surprised. 'We're mortal enemies most of the time. What gave you that idea?'

'The bike crash. You seemed to be very badly upset.'

'Yes, well . . . It looked bad, didn't it?'

Ke led Leah off the main track, through some long grass to an old tree leaning over the river. There was no grass at all under the tree, just a low hump of compressed red earth and polished humps of the tree's roots. Ke slapped the trunk of the tree and squatted beside it. Leah tried to duplicate the squat but overbalanced and fell into him. He steadied her and she sat down.

'Like it?' he said, reaching wide to present the river to her.

'Very nice,' she said, rubbing a red mark from her jeans. 'Is it special?'

'It is my fishing place. And my father's fishing place.'

Leah looked up quickly and caught Ke's eyes.

'Everybody's fishing place. All the boys and a lot of the girls come here after school to talk about things and see if they can be mighty fishermen.'

'I used to go fishing. With my dad.'

'We play Tickle the Turtle here. Want to see how it's done?'

'Sure.'

Ke moved to the edge of the bank and slid a hand into a hole in the mud above the water. 'Everywhere else it is called something else, but here – ' He concentrated, turned his arm carefully in the mud, pulled a clicking black crab out of the mud and placed it on the red earth. 'Here *that* is called a turtle.'

'Oh, I can see. Definitely a turtle.'

'It's all tradition.'

'Everything here is tradition. Looks easy.'

He frowned a moment. 'Like to try?'

Leah studied Ke's face for a moment, then shrugged and moved past him, hovering her hand above a mud-hole. 'What size?'

She ploughed her fingers into the hole feeling the mud coiling around her hand like silk. Something hard, a pebble? – but moving. A hard edge, the crab's shell? Then a sudden hot pain and she was squealing with her hand high in the air and a crab swinging from her middle finger.

Ke caught her wrist and squeezed the crab. The crab spun away but the pain was still in her finger. He put her fingers in his mouth and sucked, looking at her in apology. The pain faded to a wet and warm feeling, and she was staring at his lips.

'All right,' she said. Her ears were suddenly burning. 'Stop eating me.'

Ke held up Leah's injured finger and examined it. 'It's all right. I'm sorry. I should not have let you play stupid children's games.'

'It was me that did it, not you! I wasn't quick enough, that's all. Hey, is the crab called a turtle because the village was once called Turtle Land?'

'More than that. Tong talked about it after you got his memory going. You know about the ancient irrigation scheme on the Min?'

'Some governor cut a canal through a mountain to control the river . . .'

'Ah yes, that is the fact. But we can never leave facts alone. We have to improve the story. So, we have a fairy story, a myth. Once upon a time – maybe about 300 BC – a man died near Chengdu and his body was thrown into the Min. But this body had magic powers and it floated *upriver* and reached the bank here. Right here, where the tree grows.

'The body came to life the moment it touched

111

the shore and became an emperor and a Turtle God, using people to conquer the wild Min River as he had conquered it in death.

'The tamed Min made a desert into a rich land and a village was built with a name marking the Turtle God's rising from the river. Gui Tu Cun, Turtle Land. That's your – that's *our* ancestral village, Leah.'

17 Joan

Next day Joan was propped in bed and sparking. 'What does this look like?' She waved her arms about the room.

Leah was delighted at the recovery and beamed. 'A hospital – '

'A prison cell. That's what you've put me into. A prison cell!'

Leah's brightness collapsed. 'We had to get you into hospital. Give you some rest and – '

'Rest? Here? They clatter along the corridor like the place is on fire. The washroom is cold concrete. Everything is cold concrete. There is no television, nothing to read. Food? They serve watery rice and old meat – and that's only because someone is paying them. You?'

'That is Heng.'

'Who's Heng?'

'The man who hit you with his motor-bike.'

'Oh, the party hack. Well, you tell him this lady won't be bought off with rice porridge. I am going to sue the pants off him . . . I forgot, this is China, you can't do anything in China. Just get out.'

'They say you can leave this hospital in a week.'

'I cannot leave now? It *is* a prison cell. Why aren't I in Chengdu with real doctors, comfort, the right equipment . . .'

'Heng thought it would be better here.'

'I'll bet. Heng is just trying to keep me out of sight. He was drunk and he nearly killed me. If I talk to his superiors he's out of a job. I know what he's trying to do. What about the taxi, what about our things?'

'Tong found the taxi looking for us on the wrong side of the highway and we paid him off. Ke has gone to some friends to arrange to pick up our stuff tomorrow.'

'So we are stuck here. The way Heng wanted it.'

'But this way we are close to our village and our family.'

'Oh yes, that too. Are we sure that it is our village, and are they really our family?'

Leah wanted to kick the bed. Put Joan in hospital for two days and she is mad at everyone. Everyone! 'But you heard it. It *is* Turtle Land.'

'There may be dozens of Turtle Lands.'

'But there is that myth.'

'Yes, yes, a myth. Much the same as that stuff linking this Zhou family with us. Getting a pearl from the colour red. That sounds like rubbish.'

'It is not rubbish. You haven't been listening.'

'It sounds like another family trying to talk their way into a Hong Kong house. That student of yours, that teenage terrorist, sounds to me like another Grandfather.'

18 Ke

Leah trailed down to the fishing tree to spend some time thinking before Ke arrived. But Ke had already arrived and was skimming pebbles across the Min. Leah did not want to see him – not yet – and hesitated.

But he saw her, grinned and waved, talking rapidly as he stepped toward her. Until he saw her face. 'What's wrong?'

'The village. You really think it's mine, don't you?'

'Definitely. Yours as much as mine.' Smiling, waiting.

Leah sat beside the tree and watched an eddy coil past her. 'It's not, really.'

'Why?'

Leah hesitated. 'You live here.'

'In a two thousand year village, that doesn't matter much. Just a scratch. I know the village now, your – our – great grandfather knew it last century when there was an emperor. You'll know the village by next week.'

'What's it like, living in a two thousand year village?'

'Hey, I didn't think much about the age of the place until you arrived. You started Tong off. I knew it was old, but you don't notice it so much. It's not like living in Chengdu or Beijing where ancient pieces of buildings remind you. There is nothing much here that is old. The trailer factory is seven years old. The thatched roofs are replaced every fifteen years. The buildings are always getting added to – my father built the south wing of our house twenty years ago – or torn down to

make room for new buildings. Our oldest buildings are two hundred years, but they won't last.
Hard to live in.'

'Your father, where is he?'

'He died.' Quickly. 'No, it isn't the buildings
that last. It's the stories and the kids' games. Like
Tickle the Turtle and Tease the Dragonfly and
Catch the Cat, one chaser after everybody.
Nobody knows how long that chase has been
going on.'

Leah nodded.

'Feel better about it now?'

Leah doodled in the hard earth with a stick. 'It's
Mum. Doesn't think Turtle Land is the right
village.'

'But why?'

'I don't know. I don't know what she wants.
She's been wandering all over China to find her
father's ancestral village, following his last wish.
We find you here, the village and the family and
she suddenly doesn't want to know. I give up.'

'Maybe she's depressed. Hospitals do that to
people.'

'You think so? Maybe she'll cheer up when she
gets her things.'

'I'll be getting them tomorrow. Catching a students' truck into Chengdu. I'll have to be gone all
day. Sorry.' But he was grinning again.

'Another demonstration?' Leah was glad to drop
the subject of Joan.

'Heard from friends what happened yesterday.'
Ke pounded his knee. 'One million in Tiananmen
Square! Can you imagine that? Not just students
– factories, kindergartens, big businesses, acro-
bats, a rock band and an orchestra playing
together, even people from the Foreign Ministry.
Ah, to be there!'

'What do they want?'

'A few days ago Russia's Gorbachev had to be greeted at the airport, no room at Tiananmen. Gorbachev told Deng he had revolution on his hands. And he's right. Seven cities were marching yesterday. Tomorrow, who knows?'

Leah tried again. 'But what does everybody want? We've seen marches all over, but we still don't know what it's all about.'

'What have you seen?' Ke turned sharply to Leah as if he had only just noticed her. 'Of course, you have travelled. You must see more than any of us! What, when did you get into China?'

'Well, it was in Guangzhou on April 21, 1989 . . .' She smiled but his face didn't change. 'But there was nothing. There was only a student putting up posters about – ah – Yaobang.'

'Hu Yaobang. That was the beginning. He had been party head and he wanted liberal laws, but Deng threw him out last year. Just before you arrived he died and students marched to Tiananmen in respect for him and stayed there. Until Deng made some changes.'

Ke gazed on the river. 'They went to the compound of the leaders of the Politburo, the Zhongnanhai, to tell them what they wanted, but the police attacked them with belts.

'It's never been easy. When you arrived on April 21 there was a pompous funeral in the Great Hall but there was a great crowd outside, in Tiananmen. What did you do then?'

'Stayed at Good Field to the end of the month, saw things on TV.'

'We were starting strikes at universities and colleges to support the students in Tiananmen but Deng attacked us in *The People's Daily*.'

Leah winced. 'I got Mum into trouble in a train over that. About the crowds angry with Deng's editorial.'

'You, kid, had an opinion. Tourists should never have an opinion.'

'We saw protesters in Shanghai on May 4.'

'That was the 70th anniversary of the students' protest for democracy and modernization in Tiananmen. In 1919! We haven't come far, have we?'

Leah smiled in a touch of embarrassment. She had been seeing all this without understanding anything. 'We saw student marches at Nanjing, and at Chongqing they took over a hotel and there was a huge march of thousands and thousands . . .'

'Yes, the students there would really feel it. Deng was once the political commissar in Chongqing, doing what? Fighting corruption, that's what! You want to know what all those marching people want? What Deng, what Small Bottle won't give us? Just an end to corruption. Change!'

Ke thrust a fist out over the river. 'Democracy! No more guanxi! No more influence, no more back-door deals!'

Leah shifted uncomfortably, wondering if she should clap.

He lowered his fist and looked at Leah. 'Or something like that,' he smiled.

'It's all right. Freedom,' said Leah, trying a fist of her own.

'Freedom. And no more guanxi. Maybe that's the big thing. We want a fair chance. Deng said once that to be rich is glorious. Ha! He meant to be a rich party member is glorious. Nobody else is getting rich. Any money coming into China goes into the pockets of the party members and their friends. That is guanxi, back-door business. And everyone is affected.

'Remember Heng, the fat fool that almost killed your mother? Well, he's the party cadre, the headman that keeps the village in line for the government. But he's only got a wheat strip like the rest of us. So how is it that he has a motor-bike, the only one in the village, and the only colour TV? Because he knows important people and he does favours. So we don't get fertilizer. Someone else gets it. His son is given a factory to run. What is the difference between him and the old imperial landlord?'

Ke stopped and shook his head. 'You should stop me. Sounding off like a counter-revolution-ary! Poor mother . . .'

The laughter died, the sound drifting away on the river.

'Poor mother.'

Leah watched the light fade on the boy's face, and waited.

'She's always saying that I am growing into the image of my father.'

'He died.'

'Yes. He was a poet.' Ke plucked a dead leaf from beside him. 'You know, if you could ride a log down this river you would reach Shanghai. This is the Min, which flows into the Jinsha and that roars down from the mountains of Tibet. The Jinsha becomes the Chang – the Yangtze. The Yangtze flows past Chongqing, through the Gorges, past Yichang, Wuhan, Nanjing, past Shanghai and into the East China Sea. This river cuts China in two.'

Ke flicked the leaf into the river.

'So father, Yuzhou Guang, wrote a poem about a leaf on the river. Something like:

I see you, little brown leaf
On the dark water of the Min.
You will pass ice mountains,
Cities climbing for the moon,
Or dreaming of ancient kings.
Until you touch the smoky port,

118

Where sails clatter in the wind
And the river becomes a sea.

But I see nothing but red earth
And wheat and another year's work.
Brown leaf,
Take me with you.'

Leah looked downriver in silence. She remembered the things she had seen: the fortress city with marching students, the ant-men with the coal baskets in the misty gorges, the giant lock door, the islands of barges, the river sea, the long lines of pick-and-put cranes, the students waving their flags on a traffic policeman's tower, the old, old tree somehow living on a thumb-wide strip of bark . . .

'I wish I'd known your father,' she said.

'So do I.'

Leah turned.

'I was just a howling brat when he died. Can't remember much.'

'How did he die?'

'Red Guards. The Cultural Revolution. They killed him for his poetry.'

'For things like *Brown Leaf*?'

'Exactly like that. Father was a farmer, just like the others, but he wanted more from his life. For Mao that was treachery. Mao attacked ambitious villagers as "fat bourgeois pigs" and the Red Guards came and took father away. We never saw him again, but in one of his last times with us he told mother that if he had seen everything that was coming, he would still have written the poetry. Because that was right. And now mother keeps looking at me.'

'You write poetry?'

'I'm a student of microbiology, germs and viruses. I cannot think a single poetic thought. No, it's because I'm in these marches. Mother thinks she's seen it all before. She hasn't. China has not seen this before.'

Leah thought of the bleak nights after the funeral, when Mum crept into her bedroom and just stood in the dark, watching. 'They're like that. Frightened that you'll die on them.'

Ke looked surprised.

'My Dad died too.'

'I'm sorry.'

'Cancer.'

'It's the waste that hurts so much.'

They sat in silence by the river and Leah wondered where the clown with the flag had gone.

19 Li-Nan

The aroma of steaming dumplings hooked Leah out of bed before morning light. She bumbled into the kitchen, yawning, still straightening her shirt, and almost collided with Ke and his bucket of water.

'Hi, orphan,' he grinned. 'That's one thing we Inscrutable Orientals notice: you Long Noses never stop sleeping.'

'Don't bully the girl!' Li-Nan was working the fire under the stove.

'Yes, be polite to me, pig. What's the panic?'

'Early morning truck for Chengdu. I've got to go, got to go.'

'Oh.' Leah said the word flatly, making no attempt to mask her disappointment.

Li-Nan caught the tone and turned from the stove with a slight frown. She and Leah looked at each other.

Ke saw the eye connection and shook his head. 'Don't do that! I'll be back tonight to tell you all about it. There's no danger, no danger at all.'

Ke hastily ate three dumplings while Li-Nan parcelled four more in newspaper and string. He looked at Leah. 'Okay. Finished with the unhappinesses?'

'What unhappinesses?'

'Yesterday.'

'You had them worst.'

'The misery twins.' Ke glanced at Li-Nan. 'I'm off.' He kissed Li-Nan and for a moment Leah thought he was about to kiss *her*, but he settled for squeezing her arms at the door. 'Take it easy. She'll be better.'

'You bloody well look after yourself!' Leah called after him.

Tong dropped round for a more leisurely breakfast, but Li-Nan remained subdued as they ate. He tried to cheer up the table with a few school stories, but gave it up eventually and pedalled sadly to work.

After breakfast Li-Nan started to tip buckets of rice husks and cabbage leaves into the pig pen. Leah joined her.

'Can I help?' She was trying to delay her visit to the hospital.

'You could feed the ducks, a little rice husk, rice and water,' Li-Nan said quickly. 'Would you like to do that?'

Leah blended the ingredients under Li-Nan's eyes and began to throw the mixture about the feed hill. The ducks were confused at first and stampeded after Li-Nan instead of Leah but after a

121

few disgruntled quacks they left Li-Nan for the food bucket.

No loyalty at all, thought Leah, and scowled at them.

Li-Nan was watching her. 'Ke has been telling you about us – about my husband?'

Leah hesitated.

'That is good. We have no secrets. Ah, perhaps just a few.' Li-Nan smiled, the sudden flicker of a small girl's mischief that lit up her face and was gone. 'But you and your mother, you are like us.'

Ke has been talking . . . Leah was irritated.

'I am sorry.' Li-Nan clapped her hands. 'But I am thinking I should go with you to your mother in hospital.'

'Oh. Thank you very much, but it's not necessary.' Leah was remembering Joan's foul mood yesterday, muttering things about Hong Kong houses . . .

'You are not happy here,' Li-Nan said suddenly.

'No, no, I like it here. Very much.'

'But your mother is not happy. Of course, lying in bed all day, under the wing of Heng. She probably thinks we are stealing you from her. I know how it is, I have been there. We will go to the hospital when we finish feeding the animals. Yes.'

So Li-Nan wheeled her bike from the back of the hay store, dusted the carrier rack above the rear mudguard and wobbled down the road, with Leah seated sideways behind her. Leah spent some of the journey trying to decide whether to hold the back of the saddle or grab hold of Li-Nan around the waist. She settled for a light grip of Li-Nan's hip and concentrated on keeping her feet clear of the spokes.

Li-Nan panted slightly as she dismounted. 'You are a big girl. I think I am an old woman.'

'Sorry. Would you like me to pedal on the way back?'

'Perhaps not quite that old,' Li-Nan muttered as she pushed Leah roughly into the hospital.

Joan greeted Leah with a half-wave which died as Li-Nan stepped into the room. Her eyes tossed Leah a hostile query.

'Li-Nan wanted to see how you were getting on,' Leah said quickly. This is going to be terrible. Joan is going to treat Li-Nan like the restaurant girl on the boat and I am going to curl up and die.

'Well I'm not. All I can say is I am alive.'

'You look very well. But hospitals are bad places to stay. We must see what we can do to bring you home.'

'Thank you. But I don't wish to add to the troubles you have gathered up by hosting my daughter.'

Cold, rigid. Joan was staying behind a brick wall.

'Nonsense. She is a delight. She helps me around the farm, far better than my son, Ah Ke.'

Joan moved her eyes curiously from Li-Nan to Leah and back. 'Your son seems to think we are of your family.'

'Who knows? I hope so.'

'You do not know?'

'I am sorry, what can I say? Ah Ke thinks so. I want to believe it, but we have only a name and a village . . .'

Joan was nodding and the tension was beginning to seep away.

Li-Nan smiled. 'You brought this broken coin all the way to the centre of China to obey your father's last wish? That is very Chinese.'

'Well, we both wanted to find our family, didn't we, Leah?'

'Yes, and we have! Ke could tell you – '

'Where is Ke?'

Li-Nan grunted. 'Ah Ke is not very Chinese. He does not obey his mother's wishes.'

'He is in Chengdu, again,' said Leah.

'Like his father.' Li-Nan smiled weakly.

Joan saw something in Li-Nan's face. 'Father? What does he do?'

Silence for a moment. 'He is dead. Killed by the Red Guards in the Decade of Chaos. He was a farmer and a poet, and he said too much.'

'Oh, I am sorry.' Joan was looking at her fingers.

'Ah, it is a long time ago.'

'But it doesn't help, does it?' Joan said. 'And your son is stoking the revolution.'

Li-Nan sighed and sat in the chair beside Joan's bed. 'My worthless son.'

The two women smiled very quietly at each other and Leah suddenly felt locked out.

'I feel like that sometimes,' said Joan. 'Mine got herself lost in Shanghai with some gang running about. Bounced up to the hotel, expecting a medal for finding her way back. I could have killed her.'

'Mine paints banners and runs around shouting for Deng's head as if we are in America. Sometimes I want a dungeon with chains deep under the house, to lock my son away until he grows out of it.'

'Oh yes, yes. I used to wait by the window when the school was out. Wanted to pick her up at the gate, but I knew she wouldn't ever permit that.'

'There are rules, aren't there?'

'You have to bottle it in. When the letter came – when my father died it was a shock in my bones. When David began to die everything began to dissolve with him. There was nothing that felt solid and real.'

'Except for the child.'

'But they are so fragile.'

'Even now.'

'Even now. I thought I was getting over it after a year of study and work and you have to let go, haven't you? But China brings it all back even worse. Does it ever get better?'

'I don't know. Maybe when they stop believing they are gods and begin to feel a little afraid.'

Leah shuffled a foot sideways for balance and both women stared at her in surprise as if they had forgotten she was there.

'Oh, Leah . . .' Joan was fumbling. 'Could you go for a walk for ten minutes or something?'

'Widow's talk,' said Li-Nan with a shrug.

Leah walked hollowly down the corridor, blinking in the bright sun outside, crunching the pebbles in the drive as she passed Li-Nan's bicycle. She wiped at the mist in her eyes with a clenched forearm and jerked away from the hospital.

Why did Mum have to wait for a stranger in a strange place to talk. Why couldn't she talk with you?

20 Tong

The first group of children stopped shouting as they reached Leah and eddied around her, as if she were an old woman. Leah noticed their passing and looked up from the track to see a river of red scarves, of children bouncing, jostling toward her.

She was startled. School was out and she had not realized that she had been walking for so long. Nor where she was.

Great, she thought. You're doing another Shanghai.

But almost immediately she saw the spare frame of Tong riding slowly behind the children. He could have been herding them, driving them home.

He stopped before her, straddling the bike and smiling. 'Hello, hello.' Then he looked into her face and the smile faded. 'I have been thinking about you and the coin. You have it now?'

'Always.' But the quest was becoming tattered.

Tong swung his bike round and patted the carrier rack. 'Come back to school with me. There is a book that might help.'

The school was fifteen minutes away, almost deserted now, and pitted with dust. Leah slid past the wall of a ruined temple, a row of concrete table tennis slabs and entered a quadrangle ringed by double-storey buildings.

'My school,' Tong said with a shrug.

Leah was about to say politely that it was nice, but there was no affection in Tong's voice. She nodded and remained silent.

The building was like her own school, but only slightly. Everything, the corrugated roof, the concrete walls, the steps, the metal railings, even the rows of glinting glass, were grey. No paint, not a flicker of colour. More a prison than a school.

Tong led Leah to rooms on the second floor. 'I don't think I have been fair with you or your mother, about your coin. *I* haven't seen it, but that does not mean it does not exist. I apologise for being pompous.'

'Oh, I didn't think for a moment . . .' *This* is a teacher?

'Let's find a coin I don't know about. To the library.'

The library was a cage. The windows from the corridor and from the classrooms had been replaced by dusty mesh. The books – and there were not many of them – were ragged paperbacks with poor quality paper and fragments of covers. But one book had a vinyl cover and it looked heavy. Tong picked it up with a grunt.

'It's mine. Sometimes teachers and students want to look at it.'

Tong walked through to a classroom and wriggled behind a desk so Leah could sit next to him. 'Now, where's the coin?'

Leah gave it to him as she looked around, a little stunned. She'd seen rooms like these in films set in other centuries. Wooden desks for two – very old wooden desks, with children's carving on the sides. Maybe forty of them facing a smudged blackboard. Fans hanging from the ceiling, scarred water heaters. Nothing else, and everything grey.

Tong looked up from the magnifying glass he had held over the coin and smiled, a little sadly. 'This is not like your school at home?'

Again Leah searched for the diplomatic answer, but she caught his eye. 'Not much,' she said.

'No, and there are few like it in Beijing. I visited a school there once, polished floor and carpet, shiny equipment, new lockers and books, books, books. Outside trees and lawn . . . But that school was for children of government officials. It was a little different.'

Tong shrugged and began to draw a large sketch of the broken coin, moving the magnifying glass slowly over the surface.

'Guangxi,' said Leah.

Tong raised an eyebrow.

'Well it's influence, favouritism, isn't it?'

Tong nodded. 'You've been listening to Ah Ke.' Now the snake and the rod looked like hills and a railway.

'Is he wrong?' Leah thought she could detect a

127

thread of disdain in Tong's voice, as if he was echoing Joan.

Tong frowned at the sketch in his hand. 'Well it is a coin, not a charm. And it is very old. No writing that I know – ' He stopped, turned his head slowly, staring at the walls of the classroom. 'I have seen teachers weep in this school.'

He placed the sketch on the desk before him and leant back. 'At the beginning and later. In the beginning, because no matter how hard and well the teacher has worked he knows his life will finish here. He can forget about designing dams or becoming a professor of history . . .' Tong shook his head, suddenly angry. 'Because he has been stopped by a few officials, sometimes because of what our fathers were.

'When Mao launched his Cultural Revolution we knew what our futures were, my brother and I. Has Ah Ke told you about his father, my brother? Yes? He wrote bad poetry and they killed him for that. I wrote books of little history and they made me scrub toilets and here I am. But we were finished before we began.'

Tong sighed softly and in that moment stopped being a teacher and became a very vulnerable man.

'Our father was a good farmer, that's all. He could grow two stalks of wheat where others grew one and his family prospered. But this was before 1949, before Mao began to rule China, and in the Decade of Chaos Mao said that if you were poor before 1949 you were a good Chinese, simple as that, and if you were wealthy before 1949 you were a bad Chinese. And so was your family.

'My brother and I were ruined, but Ah Ke may escape the family curse. Who knows? Because I know my fate I do not weep in this school, but others do. New teachers know that the money they earn will only just feed them and every month this is less and less as the price of wheat climbs and the officials get richer. I survive because I have a little land.'

Tong fingered the coin. 'No, Ah Ke is not wrong, Leah. The students cry for democracy – for us that is the right to choose jobs and read *any* book. China is out there, marching with them, but it is difficult to persuade a tiger to become a bullock. Enough, enough. Now, let us find your coin.'

21 The Café

Tong stopped his bike near the rubble pile in front of the village café and Leah wiggled to her feet, using both hands to carry the book. Tong leaned his bike on the rubble and led Leah toward a table in the sun. They were very tired.

'Lemonade or tea?' Tong guided Leah past Heng, who seemed to be asleep.

'Just tea, thank you, Tong.' Leah sagged into a chair, dumped the book before her and looked up at the teacher with a guilty hump to her shoulders.

'I think we will leave it alone for now,' Tong said, and Leah nodded gratefully.

They had studied Tong's book on Chinese coins for two hours in the grey school room, looking at rigid designs, old characters, square holes, round holes. But nothing to match Leah's half-coin. There had been an interesting curve in the Tang dynasty period but the curve ran the wrong way. Finally Tong had closed the book, but they had been half way through. Perhaps they could have another look at the book in the village, perhaps they would feel refreshed . . .

'There is always tomorrow,' Tong said and ordered the tea.

'Wonder if Ke is here yet?'

Tong studied Leah for a moment. 'Not yet. He comes here first, telling the news. Just relax.' He reached out to stop Heng sliding sideways. 'But not that much.'

Heng was sprawled back against the wall with his eyes closed and a half empty bottle of rice wine touching his hand. Leah almost envied him his peace. She was too tired to think.

Oh, Dad, you couldn't know, but you've left me with a stinker . . .

'But if we never solve the coin, never mind. I am sure you have found the right family.'

'So am I.' He is still reading my face.

'We like you. Even the geese.'

Should wear a mask. 'I like you all too.'

'And if we're not the right family never mind, we can fix it. Marry you into the family.' He rolled back and laughed.

Leah flushed deeply.

Tong stopped laughing abruptly and placed his hand on hers. 'I am sorry. Do not be embarrassed. I meant nothing.'

Several villagers crowded around the café and the television was turned on. Three men sat at Heng's table and continued to argue. Heng opened his eyes, glared at the newcomers and noticed Leah.

'Ah, yes. Your mother, is she well?'

'Getting better, thank you.'

'Yes. I have ensured that your mother is receiving the finest medical care available in this county and excellent food . . .'

'So she should,' Tong said.

Heng stared at Tong stonily. 'And if there is anything you or your mother should require, please do not hesitate to ask me. I would have been most happy to have you as my guest. Are you comfortable with Zhu Li-Nan?'

'Oh yes, thank you.'

'You are a relative of Zhu Li-Nan?'

Leah hesitated.

'Cousins,' said Tong quickly.

Heng nodded, apparently satisfied. 'Well, if you find you need . . .' And he frowned.

Ke and another youth were swinging round the corner, both loaded with familiar baggage. Ke placed Joan's bulging suitcase at Leah's feet and unloaded his mate, who immediately flashed a grin and bolted for the highway.

'Truck,' Ke explained. 'Have we got everything?'

'I phoned the hotel,' Heng said. 'I made sure Zhu Ke received everything. I did not like to entrust your possessions to the boy, but –'

'What's the news, Ke?' Tong had seen the flare on Ke's face.

The anger vanished. 'You wouldn't believe it!' He grabbed a chair, reversed it and sat near Leah. 'Chengdu is under seige. The streets are blocked by tens of thousands of marchers. That's what Tiananmen must be like. Not just students, but professors, city workers, nurses, factory workers. The police can't stop us, they don't want to. Everyone is behind the students!'

Leah smiled at Tong, but he and several villagers were looking at Heng. Heng dipped his head and fixed his eyes on his glass.

'And this morning, before dawn, two of the Politburo leaders, Li Peng and Zhao Ziyang, came out to Tiananmen Square to talk with the students. Leah? Remember Zhao?'

Leah could recall the name from the Chongqing march. She grinned.

'Li Peng is a flower pot,' muttered Tong.

'But Zhao will rule China when Deng is gone. They say Zhao asked forgiveness from a hunger striker because he had not acted quickly enough in the past. A man from the Politburo asking forgiveness! And tomorrow the Politburo meets to decide what to do. Zhao has told us what they must do!'

'More money for students,' a thin farmer snorted. 'More money for people in the cities. Nothing in it for us.'

'I live here, Jiajun,' said Ke. 'I am a student.'

'Yes, and soon you will leave us to live in the cities.'

Ke hesitated.

'Everyone should be behind the students,' said Heng suddenly.

Tong turned in surprise.

'The students want an end to corruption.' Heng leaned forward, almost knocking his bottle over. 'And I say they are right! Some party cadres demand payment for permission to build a factory, or for ordering gravel for a village, and people see this and say that *all* cadres are corrupt. So I am *expected* to be corrupt. I could tell you of the sly offers I have been made even in this village . . .' He looked about him.

'But I will not. I will not cause trouble in this village. Enough to say I have refused all the offers. Let the Politburo tomorrow promise to cleanse the party.'

'Even Deng's family?' Tong was enjoying himself.

'Corruption must be stamped out. If the Politburo has corrupt members then it must clean itself. Throw out the dishonest cadres and let the rest of us get on with the job.'

A few villagers actually clapped.

And the thin farmer spat. 'Don't see much corruption round here. Nothing to be corrupt about.'

'How's your fertilizer, Jiajun?' Tong said mildly. The thin farmer shut up.

'Yes,' said Heng. 'That is a good example. We farmers – all of us – received only two bags of rice this season. And Red Sickle village, got *five* a farmer! Don't tell me there is no corruption here. Support our brave students for a better China!'

22 Lone Paddy

Ke and Leah left Tong with his book and carried the bags toward home. Leah thought Ke was strangely quiet until she got near him and saw that he was silently laughing.

'There is a joke?'

'Great joke. Now Heng has joined us. Like the police and some of the army and now some of the politicians. We're running out of enemies. Maybe new China starts tomorrow . . .'

'Li-Nan will be relieved . . . I am dead.'

'Trouble?'

'Oh, yes. I only left Li-Nan in the hospital with mother hours and hours ago.'

'Li-Nan? Is she sick?' Ke was suddenly alarmed.

'No, no, she was visiting. Li-Nan must be running wild.'

'Never. Li-Nan would know where you are all the time. She knows about me the moment I get off the truck. She's got a spy system that you wouldn't believe. Deng should take notes.'

'Sure?' But Leah felt better.

'Forget about it.' Ke waved a finger at her. 'I've got to show you something.'

He veered from the path.

'She gets frightened about you.' Leah followed him along a muddy goat path.

'I know. It can't be helped. I'll behave when this thing is over.' He stepped past an old tree and stopped, placing Joan's suitcase by his feet. Between a vegetable garden and the sea of wheat was a single paddy, gleaming red in the sunset.

'That's it. The paddy.'

'Oh.'

'I was thinking about you today, between marches. You and Joan and me and Li-Nan. I'm sorry, but I did read that letter in the hospital, the one from Joan's father to Joan, the last one. Well – '

Leah felt a tug of annoyance, but it passed.

'See the paddy, all on its own. It's ours, our monster.'

Funny little pride, thought Leah.

'When father was picked up by the Red Guards, Li-Nan didn't do much for a week. I guess we were waiting. Then she took me out here and we began to dig, digging walls, breaking up the waste-land, digging trenches back to the irrigation system. Everyone thought Li-Nan had gone a little mad and one woman tried to get me away from her. See, even now the paddy doesn't support enough of a crop to make it worth working.'

He took off the glasses and rubbed the sides of his nose where they had been. He looked like a dozy bear.

'But that doesn't matter. While we were out there working – me wasting a lot of time making mud balls – we were just *us* and nobody could touch us. We went out to the paddy and dug and didn't talk much about father, or where he was, or anything. Just about how to make that trench to the paddy work.

'And when we found out from some little grey official that father had died, well, we went out and dug and dug. Until we had been friends – "mates" is it? – for long enough and the paddy didn't matter any more.'

Ke looked at Leah. 'Understand?'

23 The Special Day

There seemed something different in the air next morning.

Ke danced his red flags out of the village, and Leah could hear the cheering from the truck as he boarded it.

Li–Nan muttered, 'Stupid boy,' but the lines of strain had almost disappeared from her face.

Tong came over for breakfast with the broken coin and a pencil. 'I am a stupid man,' he said, making Leah run the pencil lead over the break with her eyes closed.

Leah said: 'There seems to be a hollow here . . .'

'Hollow, dip, it's the edge of a round hole. *A round hole*. I should be thrown from the brother-hood of numismatists – coin collectors – for not realizing this. Look!'

Tong dropped a heavy chain of coins on the table. The coins were connected by a thick string through the square hole in the centre of all of them. 'See, the hole takes the place of a wallet in old China and all the holes in all my coins are square. Big square holes, and I should have seen that a part of a square hole is missing in your broken coin.'

'That means something?'

'The only old coins with round holes are *really* old. From 660–336BC, when other coins in China were made in the shape of spades or swords. This coin is older than the village.'

'Fantastic!' As long as that doesn't mean we have to search somewhere else, thought Leah. 'Do we know what it is, then?'

'Ah, no. Not yet. I'll keep on working on it.'

'What does it matter what the coin is?' Li-Nan said. 'It could be a broken button. All we need to do is find the other half.'

Tong looked embarrassed.

'But we want to know the story,' said Leah quickly.

'Yes, the story,' said Tong and he rode hurriedly to school.

Leah and Li-Nan fed the birds and the animals together, and Li-Nan talked a bit about Ke's father, Yuan, and little Ke floating kites in the sky on a windy day like this. She had talked a lot yesterday with Joan and she had grown to like her a lot, but today Leah must go to the hospital alone.

Leah packed clothes, toiletries and Joan's hand-bag, tied them on the carrier rack of Li-Nan's bike and rode out of the village. She rode as far as Ke's river tree, looked over her shoulder and dismounted. She pulled the letter out of the bag and sat with the Min curling before her.

Why do other people get to know Joan better than you?

She opened the letter and tried to remember what it said. There was that bit about Joan's father

136

being ill, very ill, the bit about Good Field, and the coin, the making of the broken pieces into one again. Joan had recited that much to Grandfather in Good Field but there was more, a block of scrawled old Full-Form Chinese characters that she could not read.

But she could remember now. Joan's friend, Kathy, reading the letter to herself while Joan poured the tea. The face changing, would Joan like to have it written out instead? No, no, just read it.

The old man was dying and the pity of it all was that he had left so many things undone. He had left China, never returned to see his brother, never returned to find the place of his ancestors. And he had cast his daughter away among the barbarians and there was no time to see her again. Sorry, daughter, sorry.

And Joan was crying. Hanging her head, fighting it back and angrily demanding Leah go away and make another cup of tea, but she was breaking up.

Leah folded the letter and climbed back on the bike.

You have been forgetting things like that, haven't you? Full of yourself since Dad went: Joan's dragging you off to China, Joan's trying to make you part of her Chinese family, Joan's trying to bury Dad's memory. Oh, lovely, try to think how *she* has been feeling! Mother's gone and then the father and David Waters, so quick, bang-bang. How do you cope with that? And then in Shanghai, your daughter disappears . . .

She rode a little faster to the hospital.

Joan clapped her hands when she saw the package. 'Glory be. Things are happening.'

'Sorry it's taken so long to dry.' Leah was waiting for Joan to open up.

'That's all right. I had my first shower today,

with a nurse holding my leg to keep the plaster dry. You should have seen us, dancing about on the tiles!'

It was different. She was different. 'Li-Nan said you had a long talk.'

'Widow's talk. No, more than that. Did you know she's been in Tibet, cooking for geologists?' Joan tilted her head. 'Where were you?'

Leah bit her lip. 'Bit of a tantrum. Sorry.'

'Oh?'

'You talk to anybody about important things but never to me. I might as well not be here.'

Joan looked at Leah for a long time. 'I try, Leah. But sometimes you don't want to listen.'

Leah nodded. 'Yeah, sorry.'

'But you are now.'

'Ke thought . . . why did we come to China, Joan? Really.'

'To find our ancestral village. Why?'

'But you've never been interested in that sort of thing before. When something happens you just keep on going.'

'March on, always.' Joan smiled, but with a brief shadow of pain. 'But this was different. My father was asking me, and your father was asking you. We both have come all this way to find our ancestral village – for other people. So here we are.'

Suddenly Leah realized that she was not just here for Dad. Not any more. 'But this is my family now!'

'I hope so, Leah. I really hope so. We've got ourselves involved here, haven't we?'

'That blasted coin!'

'At least we've made friends . . .'

Leah looked up, remembering her original target. 'Ke thought there was another reason for our trip.'

'The Teenage Terrorist would. What?'

'He and Li-Nan dug a paddy after the death – '

'Oh yes, Li-Nan told me. I suppose I haven't changed. Tried to go back for my father, but it is also "march on always". Yes, Leah, I wanted China to be our paddy.'

'It can be,' Leah said slowly as she sat on Joan's bed. 'It is!'

When Leah returned to the house she found Li-Nan sitting on a very old metal trunk with a hammer and chisel in her hands.

'Shh!' she said. 'I'm breaking in.' She swung the hammer against the chisel. The chisel bit into a padlock, red with rust and with a broken key jammed into the keyhole.

'What are you breaking into?'

'This is Yuan's, you know, my husband's box. It should be Ah Ke's box but if we wait for him we will never get it open. You know how it is with men.' She struck the hammer again.

'What are you after?'

'The coin, of course. Give me help.'

Leah attempted to hold the chisel steady while Li-Nan went a little berserk with the hammer, showing no care whatsoever for her trembling fingers. Then, as Li-Nan drew back the hammer for the twenty-ninth blow the lock fell open in her hand. Li-Nan threw the lid back and brushed at the dust.

A folded yellow shirt with some black stains, several calligraphy brushes, rolls of rice paper – dry and some beginning to disintegrate – books of poetry, notebooks, a photo of Li-Nan with a small boy – Ke? – and a shy man with a wispy beard, a diploma or award, a wooden rattle, another photo, curled and spotted, of Li-Nan and the shy man without the wispy beard or Ke.

Leah realized that Li-Nan was digging back into the man's past, slowing with every article she lifted from the chest.

More poetry in exercise books, a rolled red flag – what was he protesting about? – a carved bullock's head, a Japanese army cap, the fossil of a river insect, an ancient spear head, joss sticks, chipped mah-jong pieces, ornaments, a bamboo cylinder, garments from another time. And that was it. The chest was empty, black and dusty, with nothing to see or move.

Li-Nan sighed. 'Sorry, Leah. Probably someone threw it away.'

'Yes, must have. Thanks for trying.'

'We'd better put everything back.' Li-Nan reached out for the old clothes: a black waistcoat with delicate stitched designs, the cap with a little gleam of maroon showing under the dust.

Leah picked up the bamboo cylinder and passed it to Li-Nan. They stopped with their hands on the bamboo and stared at each other.

Something in the bamboo had moved.

Something small and hard had moved in the thick baton of lacquered bamboo. There had been some writing in red half-way along, but there was nothing left now but a few specks on the lacquer. Both ends of the bamboo were sealed with white wax.

Li-Nan took the bamboo from Leah, rattled it and moved away for a knife . . .

A little later Tong stood a little apologetic outside the door, the broken coin glinting in his hand.

'No, I just can't place it, Leah. Cleaned it with a little lemon juice, but it doesn't help.'

'That's all right Zhu Tong, you did your best.' Li-Nan nodded at him generously and plucked the broken coin from his hand.

Leah could not stop grinning.

Li-Nan carried the broken coin like a trophy to the kitchen, to a small piece of black metal on the centre of the table. She placed the broken coin near the black metal, then nudged the coin across the wood with the nail of a finger, reducing the space between the two pieces from a lake, to a canal, to a gap, to a seam.

'I think so,' she said.

Leah was too weak to cheer. She leaned on the table and clung to a lop-sided leer while Li-Nan crushed her, pounded her on the back and called her 'sister'. Tong fingered the two pieces of the coin, frowned an instant, then strode up to Leah and Li-Nan and embraced them both.

This is family, Leah thought muzzily and hugged them both back. What a great day. Where was Ke?

24 Scroll

Tong leaned back from the two halves of the coin and laughed. 'I am a very stupid man.'

Leah and Li-Nan looked up from their tea and Tong pushed the coin toward them. The coin was now complete but it still made no sense to Leah. There was a round hole, and to the right of the hole there were crosses, the snake and the rod, and the angle had become a triangle. To the left there was now a triangle sitting on a cross and a ladder with one side missing.

'I have been breaking my brain trying to work out what part of Sichuan this coin comes from, where it was made, what it was worth. I see the cash value of the coin in a symbol, but blink the eyes and suddenly the symbol changes and everything clicks home.'

Tong lifted his eyebrows and there was a light in his eyes. He tapped the symbols around the snake and the rod. 'That reads "Yn", and the other side of the hole reads "Ts'i".'

Leah looked blankly at Li-Nan but Li-Nan was waiting patiently.

'Or Ts'i-yn or Chi Ying, a very old town in the State of Chi, when there was a Zhou Dynasty. When China was several kings shouldering each other, before our first national tyrant. Before we built the Great China Wall, before we built armies of clay. When China was very young.'

Tong stroked the coin almost affectionately. 'I passed through Ts'i-yn once, a long time ago. Of course, it was not called by its ancient name any more, it was Tungchang, a little town on the Grand Canal. It's in the state of Shandong. Close to Jinan, not too far from Beijing. I don't know how it got to Turtle Land village, perhaps it dropped from a merchant's purse when he was on the Silk Road, bound for Rome. Well, it's not a Sichuan coin, maybe it's too old to be a Shandong coin too. Maybe it is just a China coin.'

If you look at it like that, thought Leah, it's a beautiful coin.

'But it is still a puzzle,' Tong said. 'Why was it cut in two?'

'Always you have the head of a professor,' Li-Nan said, a little smugly. 'It does not matter. It does not matter why it is cut, it does not matter where it has come from, only where it has gone.'

She tapped the black fragment of the coin, almost under Tong's fingers. 'This piece has gone to Guangzhou, to the Good Field village, to Singapore, to Australia, and it has come back. Lost with a part of the old Zhou family, and found – as the family comes together again. The rest is for some dry lecture. I am impatient to tell Joan.'

Li-Nan glanced guiltily at Leah. 'But, of course, you must tell her.'

'We'll tell her. Together.' It would be a party and the doctors would throw them all out. No matter.

'But you don't want to know the story?' Tong said.

'Story? What story? Half of the coin has seen the world and the other half – like us – has stayed here.'

'Just where?'

Li-Nan rolled the bamboo across the table. 'In there.'

Tong picked it up casually, squinted down its barrel and looked up. 'There is something else in there.'

'Oh.' Li-Nan sounded slightly annoyed. She should have found everything, completing her triumph.

'Roll of paper.'

'It's probably just a lining.'

'It has writing on it.'

Li-Nan surrendered. 'Well? Why don't you pull it out?'

'I don't know how. It's been there for nearly a hundred years. It must be dry and brittle. I don't want to pull it to pieces.'

'Ah.' Li-Nan took the bamboo from Tong and walked to the drawers. She picked up the cleaver and stood the bamboo on the table.

'No!' Tong reached for her.

Li-Nan struck to within a thumb's width of her holding hand. She stared Tong down and struck at the other end. She glared at the bamboo for half a

143

minute, gripped it, then pulled it apart. The roll of grey paper stood alone on the table.

'All right, don't touch it.' Tong held up a hand. 'Unroll it now and it will fall apart. We must make it damp and wait.'

Li-Nan looked at Leah. 'How damp? How long for?'

'I don't know. Damp cloths, I . . .'

Ke stumbled into the kitchen. Air hissing through his teeth, face gleaming with sweat, eyes flicking around the room.

'Hey, Ke!' Leah jumped at him in delight. 'We got the full coin!'

But Ke jerked back in sudden alarm.

'What's wrong?' Li-Nan was suddenly looking past him, into the dark.

'Why can't the old men see?' Ke was trembling.

Tong gripped Ke by the shoulders, like a bear. 'It's okay.'

'All they had to do today was say they would listen to us, to move against the corruption. That is all. The marches would stop. The students would go home from Tiananmen.'

Tong eased Ke into a chair.

'Democracy – it would come later. Open news, books, they could all come later. We don't want much, do we?'

'What happened?' Tong asked.

'Deng was behind it. But he has the flower pot – Li Peng – do it for him.'

'How bad is it?'

'They've declared martial law. Soldiers have been brought into Beijing.'

Tong and Li-Nan stared at each other in silence.

Leah woke next morning to tense whispers. She padded from her bed to see Li-Nan standing in the kitchen doorway, leaning angrily toward Ke, their noses almost touching.

' – got to be there!' Ke was saying. 'We've got to show – '

'No.' And the whispering became a low voice. 'It is the army now. Students cannot face the army.'

'But we've got to try.'

'You cannot. Haven't our family paid enough?'

Li-Nan and Ke stared at each other for a long time, saying nothing, Li-Nan trembling. Then Ke looked down.

'All right,' he mumbled. 'I stay.'

Li-Nan put her hand on Ke's shoulder, steadying herself, then embracing him. She was crushing him against her body when she saw Leah.

'But let me go to the truck, all right?'

'Why?'

'Got to tell the others. And I want to see what's happened.'

Li-Nan hesitated, pushing him back to examine his face. 'All right. But you take her.' Pointing at Leah.

Ke started to protest but he let it go. Leah dressed quickly and they hurried to the highway on Li-Nan's bike. The sky was lightening, high streaky clouds touched with pink, the pale wheat motionless around them.

'You glad to be a Zhu now?' Ke said as he stepped away from the bicycle.

'Yes.' She had watched Ke fingering the split coin last night, without seeming to be aware of it. He had hardly said anything.

'I am sorry to pull you into this.'

'I want to be a part of it.' Leah was astonished. It seemed that someone else had said the words.

'Not your battle,' Ke said quickly. 'Here it comes.'

The truck was no more than a speck on the dew-silvered highway. They waited silently while the flare of the red banners appeared above the battered grey body, then the flags and the crowded heads. The truck slowed. Before, the students had carried the air of a party on their way to a rock festival. Now they were subdued, even grim.

'Up here, Ah Ke,' called a tall, thin-lipped youth with a slogan wrapped around his head.

'I can't. Not today.'

The thin lips began to curl. 'It is today that we need you.'

'What is happening?'

An owl-faced boy leaned on the truck's side. 'We hear some things over the BBC and Radio America.'

'Bad things,' said the tall youth.

'These soldiers around Beijing, they know nothing about what is happening in Tiananmen. They have been kept apart, in a camp. They do not know about the three thousand starving students, the million people of Beijing, all of us.'

'What are they doing – the soldiers?' said Ke, very softly.

'We don't know.'

'But they are going to march on Tiananmen soon,' said the tall youth. 'Or why are they there? We are marching in Chengdu now, to show the old men of the Politburo that all China is against them. Come on, Ah Ke!'

'I cannot. I promised.'

'Oh, I see. Zhu Ke will march with us when the police are our friends, when we are the people's heroes. But now, when it is a little dangerous, when we must have everyone, then Zhu Ke cannot be found.'

The tall youth slammed his hand on the cabin roof and the truck rocked away. Ke watched it go from the centre of the highway, until it had disappeared.

Leah stared silently at Ke, watching tears streak his face.

'The coin,' Tong said. 'You know it was made in about 250 BC. Curiously, it was cast in a cluster of coins, the method used by the Romans at the same time.'

But he sounded flat, as if he was giving dictation.

'That's nice,' said Li-Nan. 'How about the scroll?'

'It has unrolled,' Tong said.

He was squatting in his kitchen beside a wooden box covered by a damp blanket. An iron kettle was simmering on the oven with a rubber tube running from the spout to the box.

'Let's see it, then,' said Li-Nan, holding Ke by the arm.

Tong nodded and lifted the box away carefully. The scroll was held down by two pieces of wood, but it was unreadable. The yellow paper had nibbled holes, brown stains and black streaks. The writing was badly faded and in places washed away.

'It's all gone,' said Li-Nan sadly.

Tong shrugged. 'It's not quite as bad as it looks. Water has got into the bamboo and an insect or two, but I think I can work it out eventually.'

'Then you can still read it?'

'Only what I have been working on.' Tong pulled a notebook from his pocket. '"I am Zhu Lin, head man of Turtle Land village and the father of two fine sons, Zhu Sheng and Zhu Bi. In order that it not be cast away, I wish to explain this piece of coin, this unlucky coin. To my misery . . ."'

'Well?'

'I have not gone any further yet.'

'You are a house demon, Zhu Tong. This scroll

147

must be deciphered by the time Zhu Joan comes out of that unhappy hospital.'

Leah leaped onto Joan's bed, threw her arms around her and showed her the split coin.

'Oh,' Joan wheezed. 'Ah,' she said as Li-Nan and Ke and Tong walked into her room. Li-Nan and Tong wore grins as broad as her daughter's and Ke was at least holding onto a smile.

'We found it!' said Leah.

'In Ah Ke's family chest,' said Li-Nan.

'With a scroll telling its story,' said Tong.

'If we ever get to read it,' said Ke.

'So we're now officially Zhu. Mission accomplished.'

'Welcome!'

Joan tried to say something, but the words jammed in her throat. Instead, she reached out and pulled Li-Nan to her side, beaming damply from Li-Nan to Leah and back. 'Wonderful . . .' she finally said.

'We're not much of a family to join, though,' Tong said. 'No emperors or generals . . .'

'But a poet,' said Ke.

'And there is Ah Ke to put up with.' Li-Nan threw a peanut at him.

Joan shook her head. 'You're perfect. Wonderful people. A family, I can't believe it. I must get out of this hospital.'

Tong laughed. 'That is what Li-Nan said.'

'We will get you out of here very soon now,' said Li-Nan. 'And have a holiday in our house, in our village. We will kill a pig!'

Leah wrinkled her nose at Ke.

Joan sobered and took Li-Nan's hand. 'It is wonderful to find a friend and know that she is family too.'

' "This unlucky coin," ' Tong read. ' "To my misery I find it when I am breaking new ground to the north of the village with my sons, and in finding it I destroy it. I strike hard into rocky ground and a piece of the coin flies into the air. I pick up the two halves of the coin, and my sons dig for seven days for other coins but we are unlucky. Many villagers hear of our coin and dig around us but they are unlucky too. My sons and I laugh at their greed.

' "I decide to take the pieces of the coin to the wise woman of the village to see if it is worth anything. But this woman is no wiser than a sow. It is a bad decision . . ." ' Tong stopped with a shrug. 'That is all I have done today.'

Ke picked up the pieces of coin and wandered away, examining them.

'Don't lose those,' Tong called after him.

Leah followed Ke across the courtyard to the storeroom. Since the truck Ke had been a closed box, talking little and looking at his feet for most of the time. She had been looking for a way to open the box.

'What's up?'

Ke wandered silently past a few string-tightened saws, a pump, a hoe, and stopped. He pulled an old mattock from the wall and picked some of the dried soil from its heavy head.

'Did *that* split the coin?'

Ke looked up. 'It's old enough.'

He fitted the broken coin against a chip near the corner of the mattock's blade. It fitted.

'That's it!' Leah squeezed him, then hastily let go.

Ke's lips twitched. 'One thing about we Chinese. We never throw anything away.' He pressed his lips together.

'The boy on the truck . . . it was a rotten thing to say.'

'He was right. I should not be here.'

The owl-faced student stopped in the dust inside the bamboo, a lost, nervous boy. Ke saw him from the café, hesitated and ran to him. Leah watched them talk very quickly as they approached the group around the café. And Ke was grinning.

' – told them that you are a widow's son,' the student was saying.

'Never mind, never mind. You tell them.'

'Deng has surrendered,' said Heng, and poured himself another rice wine.

'He might as well,' Ke said.

'Excuse me,' said the student, working his fingers. 'Since the declaration of martial law, there are more marches, bigger marches than ever before.'

The student closed his fingers and pounded Heng's table. 'Everyone in China is marching now! People Power! All saying down with Li Peng, step down Deng Xiaoping! In Chengdu there is no room for cars on the roads, in Shanghai students have built a Statue of Liberty, in Hong Kong one and a half million people mass in the streets! Macao is flooded by a typhoon but the people wade through the water! In Beijing . . .'

The student stopped and panted.

'In Beijing the People's Liberation Army are sent to clear Tiananmen. But they fail. The trucks are stopped – by the people of Beijing. The soldiers had been told the students were a few thugs but the people told them the truth. The soldiers listened to the people and turned back.'

Ke was looking at Heng who was studying his small glass of rice wine in the shadow of the owl-faced student.

'Li Peng's martial law has failed.'

Heng flushed, but he stretched his glass toward the student. 'As it should be. Li Peng has made a sad mistake and he must correct it. The people of China are angry.'

Tong laughed. 'What is this? Treason from the Party's mouth? Watch for a flower pot dropping on your head!'

Heng reeled to his feet and staggered back against the wall. 'You think I am a puppet? I would march to Tiananmen to carry a banner. I would do this tomorrow.'

'Well, why don't you?'

Heng shifted. 'I am too old. But if I were younger . . .'

Ke suddenly looked ill.

'". . . bad decision. The woman takes the split coin in her hands and says that it is worthless, but it is an omen. She says I have split the coin and this means that I will split my family. I tell the woman to stay with her tea-leaves and joss-sticks, but next year the River Min floods . . ."'

'It's the waiting,' Ke said, as he squelched across the field with two heavy buckets swinging from his shoulder yoke.

Leah stopped ahead and began to ladle from her buckets the manure of the geese, the ducks, the hens, the pigs and the buffalo, onto the soil. 'The marches?'

'They are going on, but they are getting smaller and nothing is happening. No army, no police, no movement from the Politburo. Are they waiting for us to give up and go home?'

'But you're winning.'

'I don't know . . . No, I can't call myself part of

the marchers any more. It's not "us" that is winning. It's "them". I've dropped out.'

'You are part of it, Ke!'

'I'm not!' Ke kicked at a clod and one of his
buckets tipped some manure over his trousers. Ke
shook his head. 'That's what I am.'

Joan sniffed as Leah sat down. 'Daughter, you
stink. More than ever.'

Leah smelt her arm and shrugged. 'Suppose I
do. It's the work.'

'Why can't they use fertilizer?'

'Because the crummy government won't sell it
to them.'

'Of course. Must stop thinking I'm in Singapore
or wherever, but you are beginning to sound like
the Teenage Terrorist!'

'Well they are crummy. You know Li-Nan has
let him go back into Chengdu?'

'What did she do that for?'

'It's got quiet now, and Ke was getting really
desperate. Can we give our part of the coin to
him?'

'Oh, definitely. That was the whole purpose,
wasn't it? Father wanted it taken back to the
ancestral village and we've done that.' Joan smiled
slyly at Leah. 'And they tell me David Waters is
getting his goofy wish too.'

Leah was surprised. 'You weren't supposed to
know that yet.'

'The scroll that tells the coin's story? Oh, I am
developing a little network of spies of my own.'

Leah laughed. 'It's great, isn't it?'

'Yes, it is. But when I get out of this blasted
hospital – in three days – we are going to have to
set about seeing some of China. Not for David,
not for my father, but for *us*. All right?'

Leah hesitated for a flicker of an eye, but that

was all. 'Okay,' she said. She owed Mum that, but she would miss Ke.

'Just to make a part of China our paddy.'

Ke trailed past the café, the rolled flag dipping from his hand.

'Hey, there!' Heng called after him. 'What news of the marchers?'

'They're still marching,' Ke said and turned a corner.

Leah hurried after him. 'Hello. Bad day?'

Ke flopped his arm over her shoulder, absently drawing her to his side. 'Not the best. How's the scroll going?'

'Finished. Tong has been using his notebook to recreate a duplicate scroll. Have a look.'

'That's something at least.' Ke poked his flag stick at the ground. 'It's coming apart, Leah. We're still marching but there are fewer people. You can see the holes between the banners in Chengdu. In Tiananmen . . . well, the hunger strikers have gone. Some are in hospitals and there's word that three have died. Students are going home and Zhao – the leader who came out of the Politburo and apologized – seems to have been pushed aside.'

Leah put her arm around the waist of the gangling youth and wanted to squeeze the sorrow out. 'Is it finishing?'

'I don't know.'

They walked into the courtyard, across the dappled shade to the scroll, where they stopped. The scroll was now sandwiched between two plates of glass, a ragged, yellowing length of thick paper. Beside it Tong's Full-Form Chinese characters marched up and down new white paper, as close to ancestor Zhu Lin's elaborate writing as Tong could make it.

Leah blinked at the scroll's black rhythm. There

was her great great grandfather, plagued by a worthless coin and an amateur fortune-teller. And a famine. When Tong read the full story to her she had felt that David Waters was standing by her side, listening. Then it had been very good, the finish of a long and hard journey, but now? How could Ke feel about the troubles of a man from another century when half his mind was locked away in Tiananmen?

'"The first flood of the Min is nothing,"' Ke said in a low, dull voice. '"We praise the Turtle God for digging the old canals and eat some of the food we have put away in the good years. But the second flood destroys villages around us and people begin to go hungry. The third year, the third flood kills our rice and wheat again and the famine begins. Thin people come to the village from the west for food but we are eating white earth and cockroaches. The thin people move on to the east and we wish them good fortune as there is nothing more we can give them.

'"One winter day Bi comes to me and says the land cannot support us all. He must take his wife to the richer land near the sea, before the hunger kills her. I argue with him but our fields are a lake after the fourth flood.

'"Bi and his wife leave Turtle Land, and I give him half of the coin I have broken. To remember us, this broken family. Perhaps he will bring it back someday. Farewell, my son."'

Ke remained staring at the scroll. 'Well, that's it.'

'Almost.' Leah pulled Joan's old ring box from her pocket and pressed it into his hand.

'What's this?' He opened the box to see the two halves of the coin nestling on the cotton wool.

'Bringing the coin back.'

Ke picked up the two parts of the coin from the

154

box and placed them on his palm. A light smile crept across his lips.

'All right?'

'Thinking. You know, the coin is China. The Politburo, the students. We did it, the Zhu and the Ji.' Ke pushed the halves of the coin together. 'Why can't they?'

25 Quest

Leah looked up from the wok and saw Ke standing hesitant outside the kitchen. Li-Nan followed her eyes and waved the chopper at him.

'Come in, come in. Don't worry, the work's all done.'

Ke took in a visible breath and stepped inside. He seemed slightly hunched.

Li-Nan's face changed. She put the chopper down amongst the onions, wiped her hands on a rag and waited.

'They've stopped the trains,' he said.

'Everywhere? Where?'

'Wuhan. That's almost everywhere.'

Leah remembered with surprise the windy city half way up the Yangtze, with the long bridge joining south China to the north. She had been there: Wuhan, Shanghai, Chengdu, Guangzhou, Chongqing, they were all part of *her* China. Almost as much as Ke's China.

'Who's they?'

'Maybe the students started it with the six-hour

march across the bridge, but Li Peng is doing it now.'

'Why?'

'To stop students getting to Beijing, to Tiananmen.' He looked away. 'We're failing, Mother. There are only two thousand students left in the square. They're too tired to go on.'

Li-Nan did not speak, just watched Ke.

'They must be supported.'

'You are marching in Chengdu again. I've allowed that.'

'Chengdu, Wuhan, Shanghai . . . it does not matter now. It only matters in Tiananmen.'

Leah saw that Li-Nan's hands were knotted into white fists. She should not be here.

'Wuhan is closed, but not Shanghai, not Chengdu . . .'

Li-Nan held his eyes. 'No.'

Ke sighed. 'I'm sorry.'

'You are not going.'

'I tried it your way, Mother. I tried to slop manure when Deng's armies were marching into Beijing. I felt I was worse than Heng.'

'That is silly. You have done enough.' She threw back her head and shouted. 'Hasn't this family done enough?'

'Would Father stop writing poetry?'

'Don't you throw Yuan at me! He's dead!'

'So I must be cautious, lick their boots all my life. "Take my money, cadre, sir, so I have the right to build a wall. Do not pay me enough to eat, because the party members must have colour televisions."'

Li-Nan whirled across the kitchen and pushed Ke violently in the chest, tumbling him backwards into a chair. 'This is my home – not a bloody meeting hall!'

156

Ke sprawled in the chair like a broken doll. He looked away, at Leah, without recognition.

'I will not be crushed by the thugs that run this country. Not again. You cannot go! Tell your conscience that you would have gone, but your demon of a mother stopped you!'

Ke moved his hand sluggishly to his pocket. He showed her a grey piece of cardboard.

The fire died on her face. 'Ticket?'

'The train goes tonight.'

She seemed to collapse over him, clutching at his shoulders, shaking him.

'Hey, it's not going to be bad. I just can't *not* go to Beijing. I would look back at the one moment when I could have made a difference in the world.'

She mumbled against his neck. 'Why couldn't you be a Heng?'

'Not enough fat.'

Li-Nan pulled her head up and looked at him. She tried a wet smile for a moment but it shook itself to pieces. 'Oh, Zhu Ke . . .' She dropped her head to his neck again.

Ke pressed his hands against her back. 'Shush, there's going to be nothing, nothing at all.'

But his face was pale.

26 Heng

Leah watched the last trace of the moon disappear behind a massive black cloud and walked heavily away from the glow from the kitchen. Li-Nan and Tong were talking through the nights now.

But Ke had been gone for only two days. They shouldn't worry. And Joan was coming out tomorrow. Couple of days and she would be in Beijing with Joan, shopping for the old friends at home: Rose, Andy, Ben. She should not feel low, or sad, now.

She could see the primitive tools in the store room, the flail, the mattock, the saws, the rumpled and empty fertilizer bags. She could smell the fresh manure in the air.

God, you're getting to like the stink!

She walked through the black village, hearing a pig snuffling, a hen flapping a wing once before settling back to sleep. A dog growled at her, sniffed the air and turned away in boredom. She had become accepted.

How long have you been here? It's nearly the end of May, six weeks from that funny kid with the paste pot at Guangzhou, six weeks from the neurotic kid that feared her mother was going to throw some sort of spell to make her Chinese. Oh horrors! Now you can control geese by the way you fling out the rice, get the rhythm of the flail as it clicks over your head; you can walk the yoke without slopping the buckets – better than Ke. How can you tell that to Rose or Ben? How can you tell that to the student in Guangzhou? No, you're not Chinese, but you're not *not* Chinese either. It doesn't matter any more.

A distant truck was quietly approaching.

But Joan will move into the village tomorrow and maybe she will sneer at the ancient, the repaired things that farmhand Leah has learnt to understand and work with. No she won't: that's not her at all. That was the little monster you had created in your mind. Maybe you're low because you're leaving China now and you're just discovering Joan . . .

Not just a truck. A truck and a motor bike.

And you don't want to leave China without seeing Ke.

Maybe, even with Joan unfolding, you're still just a little bit lonely.

Oh, fine, very good, why don't you stick your head in a bucket?

Heng's bike.

All right, all right. But do you think he has a girlfriend? Just curious, that's all, after all you have a boyfriend back home. Good old Ben, the cycle carrier.

Come on, that wasn't what you were getting at. Ben is a mate, like Rose and Andy. This is different. Leave it alone.

Heng's bike. Driven so slowly, so quietly, you had to concentrate to hear it.

But maybe you should have kissed him goodbye.

He kissed *you*.

On the cheek.

Oh . . .

He would have dropped his glasses and run all the way to Chengdu in terror. Everyone would have stared and you'd have died. Forget it.

Heng must be almost walking his bike. Why?

Leah peered along the road, toward the bamboo.

Because he didn't want to wake anyone in the village. Considerate. Considerate, Heng?

Leah stepped off the road.

Heng crept past the closed café with the motor just ticking enough to move the bike and without lights. The small truck creaked behind him, again without lights. It was carrying several bags.

Leah frowned as the truck passed her, then the smell of the bags reached her. She knew the hard, biting chemical smell.

Heng turned toward his home and his colour television.

The bags in the store room! The empty fertilizer bags. Everyone in the village was making manure because there was no fertilizer, and here was Heng creeping home with about ten bags! Something ought to be done.

Leah ran home and caught Tong saying good-night to Li-Nan. She told them quickly what she had seen.

'Are you sure?' Tong said wearily.

'I think so. I smelt it.'

'Of course Leah smelt fertilizer,' Li-Nan said angrily. 'Why else would Heng be sneaking about in the middle of the night?'

Tong sighed. 'At least he's back to normal.'

'Locust!'

But they were still just standing there. 'Aren't you going to do something?' said Leah.

Li-Nan shrugged. 'What can we do? He's the cadre, the official. He has the power. He would laugh in our faces.'

Tong pressed his spectacles higher on his nose. 'Perhaps not. Let's get some people up. Quietly.'

It was done very quickly. Leah went one way, roused the karate kid, and five other houses, Li-Nan launched a whispering campaign in the centre of the village and Tong hauled people out of bed near the bamboo.

Heng was getting under his third bag when a flicker of light caught his eye. He looked up and saw Tong, Li-Nan and twenty of his neighbours watching him. The bag fell from the truck and his eyes darted about. The truck driver stayed motionless in Heng's store room.

But Tong smiled at Heng.

Heng breathed heavily.

Tong stepped forward and shook his hand. 'Thank you, Heng Jiehua.'

Heng blinked.

'I don't know how you gathered all this fertilizer for our village. No, no, I know that these things must remain secrets. But it is a proud effort to take such a risk for us all.'

'Ah, well . . .'

'We are humbled by your generosity. Deng should know that this is what a good village cadre should be doing, eh?'

And the twenty men began to clap.

Heng dipped his head and tried to force a smile. 'I wanted – ' Groping. 'Wanted to make it a surprise . . .'

'And you have. A truly wonderful surprise. Let us help you unload and distribute the bags.'

Heng watched the men empty the truck and walk away with the bags on their shoulders. They smiled and nodded as they moved into the darkness, but Heng's farewell wave was very weak.

Round the corner a youth began to laugh, and the laughter rolled round the men, until the birds and animals in the village shrieked in sudden fright and some of the bags had to be dropped.

'All right,' said Tong, clapping his hand on Leah's shoulder. 'How do you like my foreign sister, eh?'

They all shook hands and slapped her back so she was still aching when she finally went to sleep.

Joan limped out of the hospital next day and spent most of the day sitting in the sun in Li-Nan's courtyard, watching the geese. She was astonished to learn that her daughter had suddenly become a hero. Li-Nan talked of preparing a banquet to celebrate both Joan's recovery and her daughter's triumph. But Joan looked at the strain in Li-Nan's face.

'I think we'll skip the banquet Li-Nan. I'm a little delicate still. You save the celebration for when your son comes back.'

Li-Nan protested, but only feebly. The two women spent two sunny afternoons sitting under the tree in the courtyard talking, or Li-Nan reading poetry to Joan, but they were both waiting.

On Thursday, June 1, a taxi came to the village to take Joan and Leah to Chengdu airport.

Li-Nan embraced Joan and almost broke down as she released Leah. 'Take care. Stay in touch.'

'We'll come back,' Leah said with a quiver. 'Won't we, Mum?'

Joan nodded.

'And I'll see Ke, soon, Li-Nan.'

Li-Nan looked up.

'Tomorrow. I'll find him tomorrow, Li-Nan.'

Tong smiled. 'After the fertilizer you have to believe her, Li-Nan. Leah, you tell Ke how we handle things in Turtle Land. Give them a clue . . .'

But as the taxi pulled away Tong stepped back and Leah saw Government Official Heng Jeihua. That black and angry face haunted her all the way to Beijing.

27 Beijing

The plane from Chengdu landed at Beijing airport in the late afternoon, with Joan talking about stamping about the Forbidden City, the Summer Palace, even the Great Wall as soon as they got settled. But she seemed to be a little nervous. As two air hostesses helped her from the plane she kept looking around and when she faced Leah she pulled on a painted smile.

Great, thought Leah, she's looking for trouble again. Beijing is like Shanghai, is like Penang.

But the taxi swept them along a tree-shaded road, then a broad highway lined by tall blocks of flats. The traffic was slow and light. By the time the taxi arrived at the quiet mock-imperial hotel Joan's fright mice had been put to sleep.

'Now, this is civilization,' she said, and proved it by organizing a small banquet for Leah and herself.

'Wish Li-Nan was here,' she said, attacking a fish smothered in rich sauces.

'Wish Ke was here,' Leah said.

Joan did not reply.

The next day, Friday, Joan tackled Leah over breakfast. 'You want to see Ke.'

Leah sat back warily. 'I told Li-Nan . . .'

'You want to go to Tiananmen Square.'

'That's where he is.'

'The city seems very quiet, normal. Quieter than Sydney,' Joan seemed to be talking to herself. 'Maybe it's all over.'

'Oh, it's quiet.' Leah was watching her words. 'Quieter than Shanghai on a Sunday.'

Joan flicked the shadow of a smile. 'Well, I can't

hobble all over Beijing with this leg. Going to look after myself. Can you look after yourself?'

Leah held herself down. 'Easy.'

'All right, have a look. Just have a look. If there is anything wrong, any soldier, any movement, anything at all, you get yourself back here. Okay?'

'Oh yes, straight away, sure.'

'And if you do see that Teenage Terrorist, get him to write a letter to Li-Nan. Immediately.'

Leah did not slow down until she was a safe two blocks from the hotel. She studied a map of the city over a half-pint of yoghurt at a pavement stall and found she was less than three kilometres from Tiananmen. She could get there by taxi, by underground railway, by bus, but why not just walk? She sucked up the last lump of yoghurt with her straw and set off.

There was little room for walking on the footpath. She shuffled through thirty metres of parked black bicycles, past a carpenter at work on a table, past a man selling kitchen and cycle oddments, around labourers pulling a wall down. She became part of a gentle stream of pavement walkers, sometimes overflowing onto the road, sharing it with trucks, buses and a constant flood of bicycles. But never a trace of temper, only the mild ringing of cycle bells, rhythmic dancing round other walkers, a smile given, a smile returned.

No signs of tension anywhere, no sign of thousands of people facing down an army. No trace of the army Ke had been talking about until Leah reached the tall Drum Tower. Five hundred years old and normally a tourist target, but now locked, with an army bunk cot on the other side.

A woman grinned at her. 'To protect it from the students.'

Leah found the back of the Forbidden City and walked toward the front, down a shady road lined on both sides by high red walls. She was peering at the roofs behind the walls of the Forbidden City when she wandered across an entrance guarded by two soldiers who were about to fall asleep.

The Zhongnanhai, thought Leah in surprise. Where the Politburo leaders live, where students were beaten at the beginning of the Tiananmen stand. Tiananmen must be so close . . .

She crossed the road and walked through an arch in the Forbidden City walls. Walls everywhere, red buildings behind massive closed doors. A few soldiers idling about, making sure the massive doors stayed closed. Behind those doors were palaces from which emperors had ruled China for five hundred years. It had been called Forbidden City and it still was. To keep the students out again?

But Leah wasn't interested. To her right a road ran through two arches and beyond the second arch flags were waving.

Tiananmen.

She walked quickly past the great wooden doors in the arches of Tiananmen Gate, crossed a stone bridge and stared at Tiananmen Square. A huge white woman held a torch above brown tents, tents with striped walls, big multi-coloured umbrellas and flags. Yellow flags, blue flags, white flags, striped flags and above all, red flags. And people. Maybe not a million now, but far more than the two thousand students Ke reported just before he left.

But as Leah kept looking at Tiananmen the image of the fair began to fade. The brightness and bustle remained, but there were other things. Like the banners: End the Corruption, Down with Deng Xiaoping, and – in English – Give Me Democracy Or Give Me Death. A parked ambulance, flags half-way up tall poles, police standing in the middle of the road, watching the crowd around the white statue. And a faint stink wafting across the road.

How are you ever going to find him? Leah wondered. Hey, how are you going to get there?

Between Leah and Tiananmen there was the broad and busy Changan Avenue, the Avenue of Eternal Peace, and this was set up like a hurdle race. To cross Changan she would have to get over a low rail barrier, a flood of cyclists going right, a bigger barrier, a busy highway, another barrier manned by the police, a flood of cyclists going left and another barrier.

Leah saw a subway and began walking toward the steps down. Then she saw the policeman, leaning against the subway wall, and hesitated. A lean young American stumbled at her heel.

'Sorry,' she said in English.

'My fault.' He smiled. 'Clumsy me. Hey, you want to go over?'

She nodded.

'It's easy. Come on, talk to me, just don't stop.' The American sauntered towards the subway. 'Where you from? I'm from Indiana, student here to get my Chinese right. I'm terrible but the professor tolerates me.' A smile at the policeman in passing. 'But you're not a student, too young, family here? See, it's easy. They don't like tourists running about, that's all.'

They padded down the last steps and along a wide tunnel.

'Thanks.' Leah was panting a little.

'Ah, you helped me too. You have someone in Tiananmen?'

'A cousin from Chengdu. Don't know how to find him, though.'

'That's a little bit harder. Hang around the

166

Goddess, though. Everyone goes past. Cheers.' He
jogged away.

'Goddess?'

'Goddess of Democracy. The Statue.' He ran up
the steps into the sun.

Leah climbed into Tiananmen.

28 Tiananmen

For a moment there was nobody in front of Leah.
She could look down at the stone slabs that made
up Tiananmen, the grey, slightly-worn squares,
some marked with numbers. She could follow the
lines between the slabs with her eyes, and see them
sliding together in the distance. How many stone
slabs in Tiananmen Square? Ten thousand, a
million?

Leah walked carefully into the crowds. Some
people were laughing at a youth trying to do a
Cossack dance and failing, others eating steamed
rice and little else, a team of drummers practising
their own private rhythm while a few girls sang
seriously as if the drums were not there. A boy
was reading poetry to a girl while she repaired a
torn banner. A middle-aged man walking through
the crowd, looking up in wonder.

She stopped before the statue and felt a prickling
on the back of her neck. Now it was a giant, an
impassive woman ten metres tall, knee deep in
coloured flags and holding that torch to the sky.
Celebrating, but celebrating what?

But there's no sign of Ke here.

Leah moved toward the students swirling around the massive obelisk of the Monument to the People's Heroes. The obelisk was surrounded by stone terraces and the students had turned the terraces into a command centre with tents, loudspeakers, tape recorders, flags. Some students were adjusting a large white banner near a tent on the top terrace, but they were largely ignored by the crowd.

Students were climbing onto the terraces without any opposition, so Leah nervously followed two girls. After all, she could only be told to go away and Ke might be up there. She climbed unchallenged to the top terrace, noticing four people lying inside the tent with the white banner, but no Ke.

She was now above all the other tents, the crowd and most of the flags, but she was still looking up at the statue . . .

The giant woman was not pointing her torch at the sky. She was holding it over her students, a mottled mass spreading until a group was a fly speck on a distant corner of the square. She was looking across the tents, the speckle of umbrellas, the lance of the national flagpole, past the crawling centipede of Changan Avenue, to the rust-red ribbon of the Forbidden City wall. And the stamp-sized portrait of Mao Zedong.

She seemed to be saying: 'Now is my time.'

But Leah swept her eyes around and sensed some of the immense age and power that surrounded the statue and the ragtag students. Tiananmen was anchored by four stone fortresses: a vast museum block containing five thousand years of Chinese history; the dynastic power and wealth of the Forbidden City; the mausoleum of Mao Zedong, once the most powerful man in the world; and the Great Hall of the People, where the Politburo of

China were still wondering what to do with the students on their doorstep.

Suddenly the Goddess of Democracy seemed very small.

'Hey, what are you doing up there, kid!'

Leah hunched, looked about and found Ke, grinning at her. She clambered down and grabbed him.

'Well, hallo,' he said. 'Glad to see you too.'

Leah started to smile. The smile became a grin, cracked into a laugh and she shook him.

'What I do?'

Leah patted herself down. 'Have you written to Li-Nan?'

'She's sent you, hasn't she? All the way! Well I have. Posted it and everything. The moment I got here. Go back and tell her.'

'Better write again.'

'How d'you like our goddess?'

'Great statue.'

'Yeah, isn't it? Made it out of Styrofoam covered in plaster. I helped.' He laughed weakly. 'A little. They let me, mainly because I told them my father was a poet. It was built in the Central Institute of Fine Arts and we got it here in three sections on cargo cycles. More than a hundred thousand people came to watch us put it up on May 30. That was Tuesday. How long has that been?'

'This is Friday. Hey, how are you?' Leah had suddenly noticed the weariness in Ke's eyes, the grime in his clothes.

'I'm all right.' He dipped his head. 'Maybe the Goddess is our last gasp . . .'

Two youths walked past wearing surgical masks.

Ke took Leah by the hand. 'Let's go for a walk. The masks? You can take your pick: you wear them for your health, or you are waiting for the tear gas, or because you don't want to be on a spy's camera.'

Ke pointed at a youth picking his way through students sprawling on the stone, clicking his camera as he went. Nobody bothered to stop him.

'Some kids have been here for almost a month and they are coming out in sores . . .'

A breeze lifted and a deep stench hit Leah, stopping her, making her eyes water.

'Bit worse than Turtle Land?' Ke pointed to the dull green tarpaulin walls near the museums. 'The latrines are godawful, and the doctors are really worried about an epidemic. In fact if it wasn't for the arrival of us students from the provinces, Tiananmen would have finished.'

Ke stepped aside for a small girl with earrings, sunglasses hooked in her shirt and exhaustion in her eyes.

'And her.' Ke nodded after the girl. 'Most of the leaders wanted to quit. But we didn't want to, so Chai Ling is staying on with us.'

They crunched through empty food packets and crumpled leaflets toward a village of tents. Between the tents there were others, made of sheets and plastic coats. Students were still sleeping on grass mats in the tents. As Leah watched one boy rolled groggily off a mat and another took his place.

'During the day we have a big crowd, but at night we only have five thousand. We have to think of something new.'

Leah pointed back at the large white banner on the top terrace of the monument. 'Isn't that something new.'

Ke shrugged. 'It's a new hunger strike and it's got only four volunteers and they won't do it for any more than three days. The sign says: "No other way".'

'That's sad.'

'Ah, forget it. Anything happen at home?'

Leah talked about Li-Nan, Tong, Joan, the pig that missed the banquet, the slimmer geese – and, reluctantly, Heng.

'You!' said Ke, in delight. 'Really? My corruption-smashing cousin!'

'It wasn't much.'

'It will do. Better than I have done here.'

Leah sobered as she remembered Heng's face. 'He was pretty angry about it.'

Ke looked past the Goddess at the sombre windows of the Great Hall. 'I guess they all are. The village cadres and the old men in the Politburo.'

Two white-coated men carried a girl on a stretcher toward a distant ambulance.

'But it doesn't matter now. It is finishing. Some kids want to keep it going, but I think I'll maybe go home next week.'

'Li-Nan will be glad.' Leah paused. 'We *all* will be glad.'

Ke rubbed her neck. 'Thanks, kid.'

'You sorry you came?'

Ke looked thoughtfully at Leah. Then he shook his head. 'No. You see . . . Tiananmen is the heart of China, not the Great Hall. The throat of democracy. We have shown the Politburo what the people want. They will have to make the changes.'

'Oh, yes, I suppose.'

'Yes, yes, they will! Gorbachev has seen our strength. Russia, Czechoslovakia, Poland, East Germany, Yugoslavia, Romania, our sister countries are watching us. The world is watching us – and them. They have no way to go but our way.'

Leah smiled. She could feel Ke's sudden excitement, but she could still see the dirt and tiredness around her.

'And after marching for us in Turtle Land, you Zhu Leah, are part of this.'

171

'Come on.'

'Well, it doesn't look – and smell – very good at the moment – '

'I didn't mean that.'

' – but for seven weeks Tiananmen Square has been free, and nobody's going to forget that.'

'Well, okay.'

Ke laughed. 'Never mind. Hang on, got to show you something.' He groped in his pocket and pulled out a shimmering blue egg.

Leah took it from him and felt the weight. It was like holding a small globe of deep sea water in her hand, with tiny sparks rising through the blue, and something in the centre.

'Like it?'

It was a solid piece of glass, sealing a peculiar butterfly. 'It's nice.'

'Found a man in Beijing who does glass-blowing. Thought it was an idea.'

Not a butterfly. Two halves of a coin forced apart by one swelling bubble. Forever dancing about each other, never quite touching.

'That's lovely!'

'It would have been, but for that little bubble the glass-blower coughed into it. The two halves were supposed to touch.'

'Doesn't matter Ke, doesn't matter at all.' Leah turned the egg, playing the light across her face. 'Look, could you lend it to me until tomorrow. I want to show Joan what you've done with it.'

'Oh, sure.'

'Thanks. Makes sure I come back.'

Leah half-turned, then turned back with sudden mischief in her eyes. She grabbed him by the shoulders.

'Well – '

And kissed him.

29 Saturday

Leah did not return the egg to Ke next day. Joan had booked seats on a tourist bus for the Great Wall and that was that. They coiled smoothly out of Beijing and cruised across flat farmland to scrubby hills and the Wall.

Joan had intended to climb a small part of the Wall, walking stick and all, but when she saw it rolling over steep hills like a lazy python she settled for a few photos and left it to Leah.

Leah found there were two possible climbs, the hard and the far harder still. She tackled the harder, slopes so acute that she could touch the stone paving with her finger without stooping.

When she returned, panting, Joan studied her thoughtfully and said: 'Which side do you think David would have chosen?'

Leah faltered. 'The hardest one, of course!'

Joan smiled, but her eyebrows lifted.

'Oh, all right – the easier side. The bum.'

Leah took her mother's arm and they strolled back to the bus. She was not sure how it had happened, but now she could think of Dad without pain – almost without pain – and think of him as he was, as an old friend worth taking the mickey out of. She supposed Joan, Crazy Joan, was in there somewhere, part of the cure, part of growing up, part of everything. She would work it all out one day.

In the deep of the night Leah was awakened by some distant shouting and a broken string of sharp reports. She had heard something like that a long time before. In Guangzhou, on her first full night in China.

Crackers, she thought. Someone's getting married tonight.

30 Sunday

Leah bounced out of bed to greet a wild storm of grey birds outside her window. She thrust the curtain aside and watched them swoop from the high blue sky, scudding over the orange tiles of the hotel roof, twisting, soaring, shimmering, a great ghostly animal. The birds scraped past her nose, exploded toward the sun, flashed – and disappeared, as if they had never been.

'Joan . . .' Leah was pushing her cheek against the glass, searching the sky above her.

But Joan did not move. 'It's Sunday and my ankle is giving me hell. Is it important?'

'Doesn't matter. They're gone.' If Little Swallow could only have seen that. But she wouldn't have believed it. 'It's a great day. You should see it.'

'Sorry. Maybe I'll feel better later. You go off and grab Ke and we'll feed the boy tonight. All right?'

'Great.' Leah hummed quietly while she showered, dressed and glided from the room, carrying Ke's egg. She walked past the hotel's idle taxis and ordered short soup at the very small restaurant at the end of the lane. She felt guilty but she had to admit that she was glad Joan was not with her this

174

morning. She was beginning to enjoy working things out by herself.

The restaurant owner was interested in the egg. 'That is pretty. What is it?'

'A very old coin, see in the middle. It is not mine.'

'What a pity. What do you do today?'

'First I return this to its owner in Tiananmen Square, then – '

The smile died on the man's face. He shook his head violently. 'Tiananmen is gone.'

A sudden chill. 'But the students – '

'All gone. The army comes, and they are all gone. Many dead, a great tragedy.'

Leah was not hungry any more. She paid for the food and hurried outside to the sun, the wheeling birds and the dappled lane. A little girl waved at her from her mother's passing bicycle.

Nothing was real.

Two old men sat on very low stools and drank glasses of tea while they played chess. A man pedalled slowly past with a cupboard balanced on his trailer.

No. Everything here is real. What that man said was a mistake.

Leah leaned against a wall, letting the sun bake the cold out.

All right. Maybe the army has come and pushed the students out. Ke was always worried about that. For Chrisake, in Australia they send in the cops, don't they? Army's in, the students are out. The rest of it is just rumour. The restaurant owner wasn't in Tiananmen was he? Tell Joan? No. Not yet. Tell Joan and you'll get locked up in the hotel.

Leah looked at her map.

Catch the underground railway. Goes right to Tiananmen. If Tiananmen is out of bounds the soldiers will stop you from getting off and you finish up back here.

Leah walked along the drowsy lanes to the highway, past a couple of high buildings under construction and reached the 'Underground Dragon', the railway.

It was closed.

Leah stood outside the grille-locked entrance and realized that the highway and the streets were almost deserted. There were no buses at all, no taxis.

Something very bad had happened.

She could see a haze of black smoke rising round a corner and walked toward it. She was trying to recreate in her mind the sounds she had heard last night, when she saw the jeep.

The jeep was in the middle of an intersection and it was burning. It had been burning for a long time, but now the blaze had subsided to a dead smouldering with only a single tyre showing a flicker of flame. The camouflage paint blended with the black burn smears; the bonnet lifted from the body; the headlights, the windscreen were smashed and scattered across the road. The half-doors had been wrenched wide open.

People rode their bicycles past the jeep, but never stopped and looked.

Leah walked back to the neighbourhood of the hotel with a slight tremble in her stride.

That was soldiers, she thought. And they died last night. They must have died. What has happened? What has happened to Ke?

The street near her hotel was sombre, with a few clusters of people standing on the footpath, spilling out onto the quiet road. A white-faced young man with a dark stained bandage round his head was telling his crowd something, but Leah could not hear. He was straining forward in anger, hissing every word, rolling his fist constantly across his palm. She could not understand.

She bought a soft drink at a footpath stall and tried to work out what to do.

'Hello, do you speak English?' A boy about Ke's age sat on the step near her.

She nodded, still thinking about things.

'Do you know what happened at Tiananmen?'

Leah looked at him. 'I don't know. The army.' A small crowd was forming around her.

'Some were hiding in the Forbidden City.'

Leah remembered those closed doors.

'Last night they came out with sticks and they were crazy men, hitting everybody.'

Sticks. That was not so bad.

'Then more came with guns. We tried to talk but they laughed at us and they started shooting.'

The crackers, the 'wedding' last night!

'And you were there? You got away?'

'Yes, I ran at the first shots.'

Then Ke got away. Or did he? 'Were people killed?'

'Many, many.'

'How many?' Leah was finding it hard to talk.

The youth began to talk, then a serious-faced young woman caught his arm. 'We must get it right.'

The youth nodded. 'I think a hundred. I ran before the tanks came.'

The woman said: 'It is more. I am an intern at the Japanese-Chinese Hospital, only a small hospital and there are many big hospitals in Beijing, but we had ten dead. Many more had bullet wounds. But we must go now, before we are seen.'

Leah trailed back to the hotel. She reassured herself that Ke could not be one of the hundred dead – a hundred dead! a hundred! – and he knew where she was. He would phone to say that he was all right. He had probably phoned already.

But he had not. Leah spent the rest of the day close to the phone. Joan was there. She had talked to her for hours, but she could not remember what they had said.

At night the government television station mentioned the Tiananmen violence, with a quick view of a tank rolling over the Goddess of Democracy. The army had recaptured Tiananmen Square from the thugs and counter-revolutionaries, but with a few casualties. Of 30 deaths, 27 were gallant soldiers. The others were thugs.

'Do you believe that?' Joan said. 'I don't either.'

Ke did not phone that night.

31 *The Avenue of Eternal Peace*

'I can't just sit here and wait, Mum!' Leah rolled away from the silent phone and threw the paperback at the wall.

Joan looked across the room. 'I know how it feels,' she said quietly.

'Then why can't you help!' It was unfair, but Leah had to hit out at someone.

Joan kept her voice gentle. 'How, Leah? We tried to phone the hospitals. Before they couldn't cope. Now they can't talk. We can't do anything.'

'I'm sorry. Look, can I walk around? Just a little bit.'

'It's dangerous.'

'It's over, Mum. Whatever it was, it's over. I'll

stay around the hotel, nothing ever happens around here.'

Joan breathed out heavily. 'Just stay close.'

As Leah moved to the door Joan was staring at the black TV screen. 'Wonder if Li-Nan has heard . . .' she was saying.

Leah left the hotel quickly. Through the idle taxis, up the quiet lane, around the market, and she stopped.

Now what? Walk around the block again, and again, see the burnt-out jeep and the closed station.

Or just walk slowly toward the centre of the city.

You promised to stay round the hotel.

Just a little walk. Stop at the first sign of trouble. Maybe you can learn about Ke and the rest . . .

Leah sucked her tongue and crossed the road. Past closed shops, people walking quickly, tensely. There was a burned-out bus across an intersection. No, it was a two-car trolley bus, with a wisp of smoke still curling from a window. At the next intersection there was a burnt-out bus and a van toppled sideways, then two buses and a truck. Very few cars were moving on the roads and cyclists crept about in isolated pairs.

But nothing was happening. There had been violence, terrible violence, but it had all been two nights ago. She was only seeing the signs of the past.

She wandered into Wangfujing Street. Normally it would be a major shopping centre, with thousands of tourists pouring into the shops, office workers, families, hotel builders in the crush on the footpath. Joan had planned to come here and shop before leaving China, but now Wanfujing had been shut down.

For its entire length metal shutters had been pulled over the walls of glass, locked and left. A

handful of people drifted along the footpath, as
aimless as the scrap paper tumbling by their shoes.
A few cyclists gathered near the tower of the
Beijing Hotel, single cycles and a few empty cargo
cycles. The cyclists stood on the road, talking
softly and looking at the broad boulevard, Changan, that cut across Wangfujing. They were all
standing astraddle, their bikes under them.

Leah felt her arms prickle, but she kept moving
toward the cyclists at the corner. Three days ago
she had stood on the edge of Changan, the Avenue
of Eternal Peace, with the Forbidden City behind
her and the bright fair of the students at Tiananmen. She had stood no more than a couple of
blocks away from where she was now. From the
corner she would now be able to look along
Changan, see the Forbidden City on this side of
the avenue and a little of Tiananmen on the other
side . . .

A series of reports suddenly punctured the air.

Leah stopped. She stopped walking, stopped
breathing.

They were shots. Softer than crackers – she
would never think crackers were shots again – but
with quick tearing impacts. And the shots were
still coming, echoing from the other side of a
building mass to her right.

Run!

Nobody was. But people were sliding behind
thin trees, into doorways. The shooting was
coming along Changan, toward Tiananmen. She
pushed herself flat behind a half-column and
realized that she was only protecting an ear, an arm
and a leg. She was beginning to tremble.

Maybe you cannot run. The legs won't move.

The shooting stopped. And started again as lazy
single coughs.

A tank rolled before Leah, the long barrel sniffing the air as it clunked down Changan.

Oh God.

A second tank ground slowly across the street, the deep jungle paint baking in the sun.

Leah remembered the bandaged student rolling his fist across his palm. Again and again. Tanks.

Five tanks passed Leah and were followed by a long chain of open trucks loaded with impassive soldiers. Some of the soldiers were shooting in the air, as if they were frightened of the men and women watching them from bicycles.

When the first fear eased, when the fifteenth truck passed her, Leah looked at the young faces in their too-big helmets and their shabby uniforms and she remembered. In the concrete Ji house in the Good Field village Joan and Leah had slept in a dusty room. A room owned by Tiny, the brother of Dragon, the brother who had left an army hat and a photo of a young man in uniform with a gun. Was he here?

'Look at them!' A young woman with a camera and white lips threw her hand at the trucks. 'Look at them, the filth! They have broken the covenant.'

Leah looked at the woman.

'We have been brothers, the people and the People's Army. We have been together against the Japanese, against Chiang's warlords, together in the hunger. But now it is finished!'

The woman swung her camera forward like a gun and ran, crouched, to a narrow tree ten metres from the passing trucks.

A few minutes later a truck slid across the street, and stopped. The cyclists looked at the youths with guns and the youths stared down at the cyclists. Suddenly the cyclists wheeled away and fled along Wangfujing, leaving the walkers standing bare, behind trees and in doorways.

181

And in that moment Leah stared at a soldier who was staring at her. The soldier stood in the truck with his hand on the side and his rifle pointing at the sky.

Leah's body cringed.

She was certain that the soldier was about to lower his rifle, point it at her. And fire.

Please, she thought. Please, Tiny.

Then the woman with the camera started to take pictures. The soldier looked down and a faint frown crossed his face. He lowered his rifle.

The woman scrambled to her feet in alarm.

The soldier levelled his rifle.

The woman ran, the camera banging about her right hip, staring at Leah, mouth wide with her lower lip wet. Leah could hear her now, the sighing pants, the slap of the soft shoes on the road. A whiff of bitter sweat and she was past, a hair comb glinting in the sun.

The soldier fired, only once.

The woman crumpled. She took a step, the ankle twisted, the knee skewed, the leg buckled, the body folding. Her arms flapped as she fell, but her face slapped heavily onto the road. The camera rolled into the gutter.

The truck rolled on and the soldier stared at the woman with a blank face.

A cargo-cycle man rode fast back down Wang-fujing, turning, skidding to a halt beside the woman. People rushed from their shelters to lift the woman to the flat-bed of the cargo-cycle, to retrieve the camera. The cyclist rode off, with men running around the woman.

Leah was left alone at the side of the road, numb and staring at the spreading stain on the road. After a long time she shuffled back to the hotel like a very old woman.

She could not tell Joan.

32 Night

Leah lunged across the bed to catch the phone on the second ring. 'Yes?' She rolled out of the morning glare with a nervous quiver. The nightmare was about to finish!

'Joan Waters?'

She wanted to hurl the phone against the wall. Not Ke, an Australian man in a hurry.

'No. She's in the shower.'

'Doesn't matter. You're Leah?'

'Yes.' Not Ke, but perhaps it's news from Ke.

'I'm Jim Ellis from the Australian Embassy. I am in your hotel, in the foyer. Can you pack and get here in about five minutes?'

'Yes . . .'

'Good. We're getting you out.' Jim Ellis hung up.

When Leah told her Joan whimpered, 'Oh my God' twice.

Yesterday Joan had told the embassy where she was, just in case things got serious. She was told to stay in the hotel, that there had been a massacre in Tiananmen Square and soldiers were still shooting people in Changan Avenue. It could not get much more serious. So Joan had waited for Leah for a terrible two hours and when Leah finally arrived she seemed to be in shock. No, she hadn't seen anything, only some burning buses in the distance, and had Ke phoned?

Today things must have got more serious. Joan dressed in three minutes while yelling constantly at Leah. Leah scuttled into the bathroom, scooping up everything, into the cupboards, clothes off the hangers, spare shoes off the bed. They were not in the foyer by five minutes but by less than eight. Joan thrust her case at an angular sandy-haired man as he tried to greet her, and paid the bill as if the hotel was about to burn down. They joined a wide-eyed couple in a large car.

'Sorry about that,' Jim Ellis said. 'We're collecting all our nationals, getting you all safe. All the other embassies are doing the same thing, the British, the Americans – some soldiers fired at the American Embassy. The government is sending up a Qantas evacuation flight to take you out tomorrow.'

'But I can't reach Ke,' Leah said faintly.

'Ke? A friend?'

'A cousin.' No, that sounded too distant. 'And a friend.'

Jim Ellis looked sideways at her. 'A student. At Tiananmen?'

She jerked her head up. 'Yes.' But his face denied any hope.

'No, I cannot help you. Perhaps the Australian students at the embassy might know of him. Ask around. The hotel knows where you've gone. He might phone you at the embassy.'

Leah remained silent as the car glided along a deserted highway and crawled through a guarded and manned gate. They climbed out of the car and Jim Ellis drove back to central Beijing. Inside the door clusters of tourists drank tea and ate biscuits. Some of them seemed to be excited, but most looked tired and unhappy.

'I've lost five thousand dollars, just like that. Bang goes my holiday. Only been in China a fortnight.'

'Hah! At least you've seen something. I arrived on Sunday. I may have lost ten thousand dollars, but I'm going to get my lawyers onto my travel group if they don't give me my money back.'

'But this is an experience! You'll always remember being evacuated from a city gone mad! You'll never have something like this again in all your days. It's thrilling!'

'My travel group are still in China. They left Beijing for Mongolia yesterday, said it wasn't dangerous. I left them. They're mad.'

'Do we have to pay for the evacuation flight?'

Leah watched the two phones at the receptionist's desk. One was for people trying to make an outside call, to a Beijing suburb or to Australia. People were almost always using it, but they were rarely successful. The other phone was for the receptionist to call out on government business, or for calls coming in.

After a while she approached the receptionist, a weary Chinese woman. 'Ah, excuse me, I'm expecting a call.'

'Oh yes.'

'From Zhu Ke, a student.'

The woman softened. 'I understand.'

'Well if anyone – anyone at all – asks for Leah Waters, or Zhu Leah . . . well that's me.'

'I hope for you.'

A little later the tourists drifted toward the front door.

Jim Ellis approached Joan. 'We're moving the tour groups to safe hotels on the outskirts of the city. Would you like to go with them? Or you can stay with the students, here?'

Joan swept her hand towards the front door. 'I think we will – ' And then she saw Leah staring at the phone. 'Stay here.'

'Be a bit rough.'

'That's all right.'

When the tourists had gone the students spread out and relaxed a little. They began to talk.

185

'Sorry about this,' a tall boy pulled at a black T-shirt. 'I just walked in on Sunday to ask what was happening. That was it. They wouldn't let me out. I couldn't go back to Beijing University, so this is all I've got.'

'The army came to the universities. They shot people.'

'There was a sheet carried from Tiananmen. Was red, soaking. Kids were breaking down.'

'I was in the dormitory and some of the Chinese kids were outside the window making up Molotov bombs to throw at the next tank or truck, no matter what.'

'I don't want to go home! I want to stay and help them fight.'

'Your parents will love that.'

The students and Leah made sandwiches for dinner, worrying about an Australian student's Chinese fiancée.

'Trouble is, the army is sealing off the city. Can't get into the railway station without something that shows you *aren't* a student.'

'They are going to come down on people.'

There was a collection of RMB currency. People's Money for the trapped Chinese student.

A few students carted in some cushions and sleeping bags from an outside storeroom and spread them across the lounge. They were all very tired but few slept. The talking began again.

'Can't phone Australia at all now.'

'Sorry kid, didn't know this Ke boy. You're just one of us. So many friends we've lost, and you never know.'

'They were planning this for weeks, weren't they?'

'Yeah. But *all* of it. Jesus.'

'Don't know. Maybe – '

'It started on the Friday night, y'know. Five

186

thousand soldiers, unarmed, jogging up Changan to Tiananmen.'

'They were stopped.'

'They were meant to be stopped. They didn't put up any sort of a fight. They made an excuse for Sunday.'

'A doctor said the body count in the Beijing hospitals was one thousand five hundred.'

'"Body count?" Christ, it wasn't a war.'

'No, it wasn't, but tell Deng that.'

Leah sat back on a large sofa and after a while the mutterings of the students became a picture. She was in Tiananmen on the morning of Sunday, June 4 1989 . . .

Clusters of round lights pick out flashes of red in the rippling movement across the Square. The Monument of the People's Heroes is alive with banners, weaving torches, but the surrounding buildings – the museum, Mao's mausoleum, the Great Hall – hunch over their shadows. The students hear distant shooting and some sit in their tents to wait.

A few minutes before midnight youths run in from Changan, shouting: 'Live fire! Live fire!' Troops have attacked a citizens' barricade of blazing buses to the west, firing to kill. The students' leader, the tiny girl Chai Ling, gathers people round the Goddess, swearing them to defend the Square to the death.

A single armoured troop carrier swings into Tiananmen, scattering students as it runs past Mao's mausoleum, the Great Hall, and away along Changan. A second carrier is attacked with petrol bombs and retreats to the west, slow and on fire. A third carrier is caught on a road divider and set on fire. One of the two crewmen is killed as they both try to escape.

Troops arrive on the northern and southern

edges of the Square, roads blazing behind them. Police burst from the Forbidden City and attack people with sticks.

Students appeal to the troops on Changan, but the troops seem to be unable to understand them. At 2.40 a.m. they lower their rifles and fire heavily into the mass of students. Some of the soldiers are laughing as they step over the bodies. Behind the troops, tanks and troop carriers form a single line.

Chai Ling makes a last appeal to the troops over the loudspeakers and is ignored. She then tells the students that only with their sacrifice can they save China. They begin to sing.

Troops now surround Tiananmen, on the northern edge, the steps of the museums, behind the mausoleum, in the Great Hall. Light gunfire comes from all sides, one of the hunger strikers, Hou Dejian, appeals to the students to hand in any weapons they have collected. Guns and clubs are piled on the top terrace of the monument.

At 4 a.m. Hou and another hunger striker begin to negotiate with the army commanders to gain a safe passage for the students through the lines of troops. The lights of Tiananmen are turned off.

In the darkness Hou is promised passage past Mao's mausoleum, but many students do not want to leave. Students burn rubbish for light.

At 4.30 the lights come back but the circle of troops has tightened. Students filter toward their promised passage, but troops behind them storm the Monument, clubbing students within reach. Tanks tear through tents, a girl runs between two tanks and disappears. Troops march toward Mao's mausoleum, firing as they move.

At 5 a.m. Chai Ling leads the student column through the troops, but the students are later attacked by troop carriers. Several students are crushed.

'Then they cleaned Tiananmen with bulldozers and a fire. Did you see the black smoke?'

Leah leaned into the warmth of Joan's body and slept when the last bleak mutter had died.

She woke when a brash woman strode across the lounge, her necklace tinkling on her neck. 'This is appalling! Look at the mess. And this is supposed to be an embassy!'

After a breakfast of bread and cheese and tea an open truck stopped outside the embassy door and was loaded with bags, suitcases, rucksacks and people. Leah looked at the abandoned receptionist's phone for a moment, then turned away and climbed into the truck. An Australian TV cameraman filmed the truck as it moved away and someone suggested that the students smile for their parents, for certainly the film would get home before they did. Leah tried and failed.

The truck rolled away from the quiet city toward the airport and passed a small encampment of soldiers. Some of the soldiers pointed at the truck and laughed.

Joan stared at them in recognition. 'It's the mob,' she said dully. 'Again.'

Leah turned away and hauled Ke's egg from her pocket. She could see the two halves of the coin twirling in the blue together.

The coin had been so many things: a secret, a treasure, a family keystone, and an accident. What was it now? Just a frozen butterfly?

No. Not a butterfly.

Leah lifted the egg to her eye, saw the split coin, almost one coin again, with the marks of a very old town by the Great Canal. It could have been Good Field village, or Turtle Land, or Shanghai, or Beijing. It could have captured the image of a warm, gentle China. But it had been torn apart by a cough, by an eruption of sudden violence and

189

maybe it would never heal. She saw the coin with Ke's eyes.

Joan took the egg from Leah's hands and held it. 'Pretty . . .'

'Ke said . . .' Leah shrugged, 'it was China.'

'Well . . .' Joan put her free arm around Leah and crushed the girl into her side. Leah looked up and saw that Joan's eyes were filling.

'Mum . . .'

'Poor, sweet Li-Nan.' Joan whispered.

'Oh Jesus,' Leah closed her eyes. 'Oh Jesus.'

The two women clung together in the back of the crowded truck.

ABOUT THE AUTHOR

Allan Baillie was born in Scotland in 1943, but has lived in Australia since he was seven years old. On leaving school he worked as a journalist and travelled extensively. He now lives in Sydney with his wife and two children and writes full time. He is the author of seven highly acclaimed novels for children, and a prize-winning picture book:

Adrift (Shortlisted for the 1985 Australian Children's Book of the Year Award, and winner of the 1983 Kathleen Fidler Award)

Little Brother (Highly commended in the 1986 Australian Children's Book of the Year Awards)

Riverman (Winner of the 1988 IBBY Honour Diploma [Australia] and shortlisted for the 1987 Australian Children's Book of the Year Award)

Eagle Island

Megan's Star (Shortlisted for the 1989 Australian Children's Book of the Year Award)

Hero (A Children's Book Council of Australia Notable Book, 1991)

Drac and the Gremlin (Winner of the 1989 Australian Picture Book of the Year Award).

Allan researched the background for *The China Coin* during a journey through China with his family in 1989, and he was in Beijing while the dramatic and tragic events were taking place in and around Tiananmen Square in June that year.

MORE GREAT READING FROM PUFFIN
☆☆☆☆☆☆☆☆☆☆☆☆☆☆☆☆☆☆☆☆☆☆☆☆☆☆☆☆

Megan's Star   Allan Baillie

Kel has rare powers and knows that Megan has them too. But as they explore their capabilities, Megan realises she must soon give up all she knows, for there will be no turning back.

Shortlisted for the 1989 Australian Children's Book of the Year Award and the 1989 NSW Premier's Award.

Eagle Island   Allan Baillie

When chance brings Col and Lew together on a lonely island in the Great Barrier Reef, their encounter turns into a deadly game of hide and seek.

Hero   Allan Baillie

A powerful adventure story based on the Sydney flood of 1986 from a highly acclaimed author.

A Children's Book Council of Australia Notable Book, 1991.

Firestorm!   Roger Vaughan Carr

A gripping novel about the terrifying and destructive fires of Ash Wednesday and their effect on Ben Masters and his family.

Shortlisted for the 1986 Australian Children's Book of the Year Award.